PRISON BAE

DENISE ESSEX

B. LOVE PUBLICATIONS

I dedicate this book to everyone who has supported my literary career thus far!

ACKNOWLEDGMENTS

I'd like to acknowledge:

My family: Thank you for allowing me to take up space as an author.

BLP: Thank you for your advice, support, and encouragement.

Editors and proofreaders: Thank you for your patience and all the invaluable information you share!

My accountability partners: Thank you for motivating me with your inspiring goals and holding space for mine!

Me: Thank you for *continuing* to do it, despite your fears. I see you, Goddess!

Readers: Thank you for taking time from your life to play in my world!

PREFACE

Dear Reader,

Thank you for your interest in my current release. There are brief mentions of sexual assault. If you find this topic triggering, please take care of yourself while you engage with my work.

If you enjoy what you read, **leave a five-star review** on **Amazon, and a positive review on Goodreads, and TikTok**. Also, be sure to recommend it to your friends. **Follow me on Amazon and** sign up for my mailing list so we can keep in touch.

Mailing list

With Love,
 Denise Essex

Sweet Heat
DENISE ESSEX

1

S ade

I COULDN'T BELIEVE I GOT THE FUCKING COUNTY HOSPITAL FOR my clinical rotation! Jennifer got the women's clinic in the 'burbs where they did breast and gynecology exams. There was a coffee trolley that delivered free coffee to patients and employees each day. Imani was placed at ENEP's (Everest Northern Engineering Program) medical center. Her site was located near mine because the medical center was only open during the day.

Patients and students who needed care evenings and weekends would be seen at the county hospital. Imani was over the moon because ENEP's medical center was rumored to service a few celebrities. *Typical.* She looked like a doll. Her hair, makeup, and lashes were always flawless. I enjoyed a good beat like the next girl, but with eight a.m. classes that lasted until evening, there was no way

I would attempt to keep that up while enrolled in one of ENEP's most intensive programs.

Brandon was selected for the children's hospital, which was the equivalent of working in an arcade. I couldn't be too upset though. While I was one of the top students in my cohort, Brandon was the smartest person in our entire class. The children's hospital seemed like an amusement park with all the bright lights and animal therapy dogs, but I quickly learned it was also hard as shit.

Unlike the rest of our ultrasound patients, pediatric patients were targets who moved. They couldn't sit still for more than five minutes. I'd posted pediatrics as one of my top three clinical sites for the Wishlist the clinical director had us fill out. She explained that we weren't guaranteed placement at any of the locations we selected.

Miss Coleman, our clinical director, was in her late thirties, but her youthful appearance made her look the age of a college student. I could tell she had to remind the hospitals, students, and some of her colleagues that she knew her job. It wasn't her fault Black didn't crack. She was overly thorough and brought that same energy when she handed out my treacherous site.

"I'm basing your clinical placement on several considerations with space being the ultimate determining factor. Is your potential clinical site taking students this semester? Are they taking two students or only one?

"The next consideration is your ability. If you want the children's hospital, like so many students do, you need to be as adept as a surgeon with the demeanor of a cruise director.

"A four-year-old patient does not care that you are searching for a tumor in their belly. Yes, I said belly. Do not say abdomen to a pediatric patient, because you won't get very far. You have to be silly with them, attentive with their parents, and professional with the radiologists who diagnose the patient based on your ultrasound. In all, you need to be at the top of your class to land a rotation there.

"The last factor is temperament. Are you laid back? You might not do well at a fast-paced urgent care or in an emergency room setting. Are you energetic and good with people? Geriatrics may not be the place for you. You might be entertaining to some of the older patients, but chances are you'll be bored out of your mind.

"I'll hand out your clinical placements at the end of the day. Otherwise, none of you will listen to a word I say during the lecture. And what I'm covering today is important. Today's lecture is on how to properly explain your ultrasound to the assigned radiologist."

Miss Coleman was right. Once I got my clinical placement, I was stressed and distracted. I'd heard horrible things about the county hospital. One of the upperclassmen mentioned how she prayed she would get a job offer at the county hospital once she graduated because the pay was almost double when compared to other sites.

She went on to say rather nonchalantly, every day she left her shift, she was convinced she would be shot in the back of the head. *Bish, what?* And she divulged that they do exams on prisoners there. *I'm too damn pretty for this shit.*

On the walk to my car, I mumbled under my breath and slammed right into two of the most good-looking men I'd ever seen.

"My bad, sis. You good?" the tall one with the deep voice asked in response to my grumblings.

"Damn!" I hadn't intended to say the curse aloud, but they were fine as hell. I'd heard about the big one. D, the dicknatist, was what the girls in my dorm called him. He smiled and showcased the type of beautiful teeth that made a girl want to bear his children. "I mean, yes. I'm OK."

"Cool. Be safe out here, young one. It's dark. Matter fact, need us to walk you to your car?" his friend asked. He gave me more charm than I felt was necessary.

"Uh, I don't know you." My voice was laced with an attitude to show I could hold my own. I walked with a smile all the time, which would eventually get me into trouble. Especially since I'd been assigned to the county hospital.

"I'm Rashad. I can't speak for D, but my moms raised me right.

She'd kick my ass if I left you out here without making sure you got to your vehicle safely."

"Sade."

"Like the singer?" D asked, impressed.

"Yes."

We continued to walk the extended path of the lush ENEP campus in silence.

"Woman of few words, I see," Rashad offered as they crossed the street with me toward the overflow parking lot. It was barely lit, and I realized it was a good thing I hadn't walked alone. Although I didn't know them, my gut said they were trustworthy.

"I'm not shy or quiet, for that matter. I just don't know you, that's all."

"If you're named for the singer, do you have her full name?" D queried. He was distractingly handsome. His lashes were black and longer than mine. D had a smile that was either the result of expensive dental work or highly favorable genetics.

"Whatchu mean, man? The woman's name is Sade. Like Prince and Elvis. Just Sade," Rashad interjected incorrectly.

"No. He's right. My name is Folasade. Just like the singer. Her first name is actually Helen. Her middle name is Folasade. My dad had a major crush on her. So much so, my mom didn't mind giving me her name."

I arrived at my car and felt relieved I was in good company.

"Thanks, Rashad and D. It was nice to meet you. Most upperclassmen ask for my number without knowing anything about me. Then they turn around and text me 'wyd' and ask for pics. Or they send pictures of their dicks. Why do guys think that's a turn-on?"

I could see that they tried to keep serious faces, but they simultaneously burst into wild laughter.

"D does that shit all the time," Rashad said.

"Stop fuckin' playin', Rashad. You know I'm off the market." He returned his gaze in my direction and added, "Anyway, I'm sorry people aren't treating you like a human. These clowns are super immature for that. You seem like you got good energy to me."

I smiled at him and nodded my appreciation.

"We've escorted you to your ride, so we're gonna let you go. See you around, Folasade. And let us know if you need anything. Or if them fuckboys take it too far, OK?"

"Yeah, OK." I had more pep in my step. I'd momentarily forgotten about my clinical placement fiasco until my phone chimed. It was an email from my clinical director with the contact information and arrival instructions for my first day.

2

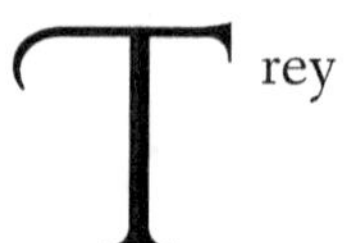

I deserved to be locked up. Not for the crime, because that was fucking necessary. But on a subconscious level, I craved discipline. I was the type of person who both hated and desperately needed structure. There was no alternative option to structured living here.

The schedule was predictable. We were counted like cattle numerous times throughout the day. It was a mandatory practice that taught us to do as we were instructed or be severely punished. I was determined to do my time, possibly less time for good behavior, without adding anything to my sentence. Therefore, I did what I was supposed to.

The dynamics in prison were like high school times ten. Everyone had to belong to a group to survive. There were the racist white boys who hated Black men. There were militant Black men who hated white men. Then there were men who were openly with male partners but did not identify as gay. They confused the hell out of me when I got here, but I quickly realized what they did was none of my business.

There was also a decent size group of the almost famous guys who were rappers or athletes on their way to the league. And then there was me. Only a few of us got a pass to move between groups. I was granted that privilege because I was naturally gifted at putting people at ease. I also made sure to break a man's jaw who tried me on my first day.

I didn't go look for trouble, but when it found me, I capitalized on the opportunity to make an entire production out of my response. The guy was twice my size, so when I hit him once and put him to sleep in front of everyone during chow, I never had to prove myself again.

It helped that I had the charm to finesse other people to believe I was their best friend. These were simply transactional relationships. My only real friend was my boy Monte from the neighborhood, and we hadn't spoken in years.

Lock-up is not exactly as it appears on television. It's not *always* dangerous. I'd gotten lucky and was sent to a low-level security prison. By the grace of God, my sentence was five years. It helped that before the incident I'd never been in trouble. I had good grades and received a full ride to ENEP for architectural design.

My teachers gave character references for me. It was the type of affirmation most people aren't fortunate enough to hear while they're still among the living. They said things about my character I suppose would go into a reference for an important job or in my obituary. I held mixed feelings about the experience. It was during this time that my prison sentence started to feel like death.

My professor from Jiu Jitsu may have caused more harm than good during his character reference. He recounted a story about me from middle school when some assholes bullied a kid named Jacob, who walked with a limp. I talked to Jacob because he could draw anime better than anyone I'd ever met. They gave him a hard time, so he asked if I could look out for him. I told him no problem and that he should just tell them I was his cousin. If he did that, they would leave him alone. But they didn't.

One day after school, two boys twice his size and a little taller than me had pinned him against the back of the building. When I approached, they punched him in the gut. I don't know what on the ancestors' green earth would possess someone to physically abuse another human with a visible disability. I wanted to ask them, 'Who the fuck raised you'?

That day was when I experienced my first blackout. I lost time and beat the shit out of both boys. I couldn't remember what happened, I just know I snapped. I broke one of the kids' jaw and the other's nose. My professor didn't mention the blacking-out part.

What he did relay was how the principal of my school believed my intentions were righteous. The principal decided training at the Jiu Jitsu academy would be mandatory for me. He said I needed to learn to manage my emotions better.

Along with my training, I became the student speaker for the anti-bullying campaign at my school. Photo ops with the school district, articles in the newspaper, and interviews were additional aspects of my new position. My professor's intention of mentioning that story was that he agreed with my principal—I didn't have an evil or malicious bone in my body. He said he'd never met anyone who forgave as organically as I had.

I didn't hold a grudge against those boys or hold the fight over their heads. The two bullies traveled with me and Jacob to anti-bullying conferences. We became good friends and a living example of how relationships could improve with effective communication. I noted the moment the judge tuned my professor out. It was when he heard what I did to their faces.

Before all of this, I had two things on me at all times—a sketch pad and a pencil. I drew a shitload of buildings. Some were realistic and some were more of an extension of my imagination. I created plans for a house I said I would build for my mom when I was only sixteen. Every kid in the neighborhood said they would buy a house for their mom when they finally made real money. I had the intention of writing. I knew exactly what my mom liked, and I drew the plans myself.

As far as architecture, I hadn't drawn any structures since I got locked up. I lost my passion for buildings. I was stuck in one with seemingly no end in sight. I still enjoyed the art, but I shifted to sketch living, breathing inspiration. I drew the grass. I sketched other inmates or their ladies from pictures they had. They got major points when they sent the renderings with sensitive messages attached.

The portraits gave me even more flexibility among the groups here. Sketched pictures for somebody's lady on the outside wasn't reserved for a specific race or ethnicity. It kept my brain from the trap of boredom because sometimes it felt like I had too much free time. People either lifted weights or read books. Along with drawing, I did both.

I watched other inmates choose food as a companion and as a way to pass time. They let themselves get fat, but not only was I too young to let myself go, I knew I would get out eventually and I had to make sure I still got ass. There was no way I would fall off just because I had a little time. Working out and reading kept my mind feeling free even though my body wasn't.

I got around to consuming all those recommended books most people kept copies of but didn't actually make the time to read. *The Autobiography of Malcolm X, the Miseducation of the Negro, The Coldest Winter Ever, Our Eyes Were Watching God* along with a ton of self-improvement books on self and anger management. The most memorable books were the ones on emotional intelligence. Until I was forced to sit still, I had no idea how inadequate I was at understanding my emotions.

Surprisingly, books got me into the pettiest conflict. Some of the other inmates would say I thought I was better or smarter than them simply because I had a paperback in my hand. The most frustrating accusation was when they'd say, 'We know you ain't over there reading'. Did they think I sat with a book for hours to pretend to read? To impress them? Pretending to read a book took much more effort than actually reading it.

"Edmund, your turn for the phone."

I needed to call home, but I didn't want to. I missed my family and I wanted to thank them for their support. But calls home were emotionally draining. A conversation with my family was the opposite of what I needed to stay sane and keep my mind clear. Especially since my actions divided the family. My brain would spiral about one misguided question or one piece of gossip. My Aunt was at my mom's for a visit one time when I called. She let it slip that my other aunt said I tore up the family and that I should have gotten more time. It took me months to recover from that one phone call.

"Skip me. I'm good."

"You sure?"

"Yeah, man. I'm good."

I grabbed a scrap of paper from the table and put my focus on sketching the hummingbird by the window.

3

S ade

I TOOK A DEEP BREATH AND TRIED TO PRETEND THAT I WASN'T about to vomit. Today was my first day at the county hospital. I had changed my hair five times. I didn't want my natural hair out while I was on-site as an intern. Although ultrasound was not the same as nursing, there was a chance that someone's bodily fluids could get on me. This would be completely different from practice in the lab on campus.

So, I decided to put it up, but my bun looked messy. Not the effortless, on-purpose messy, but the 'girl, do you love yourself' kind of messy. I was blessed. I was one of those girls who didn't need to put much effort into my appearance and men still found me attractive. I was taller than most women at five feet nine inches with the wide curves of a brown goddess.

I was aware that I was not everyone's cup of tea, because people constantly gave me backhanded compliments and thought it was perfectly acceptable. They mentioned things like I have such a pretty *face* or that I could be a *plus*-sized model. The plus-sized always came out in slow motion because I was so fucking sick of hearing it. I was two hundred and seventy-eight pounds and I had zero shame about it. Men certainly had no problem with my size. I embraced my thick build in high school. I had the cheerleaders' boyfriends begging for my attention publicly and behind closed doors.

I decided on a top knot bun in the front and left the back half out. I'd done a twist out last week, which left it quite curly. I applied lip gloss and eyeliner and called it a day. Regardless of how big and unmotivated society labeled me, I did yoga every morning and sometimes took a walk to the smoothie shop for my morning green skin-poppin' drink. That part of my morning routine was the only thing that kept me from a complete meltdown. The blaring music and bass from my car speakers on the drive-in helped too.

Everyone was extremely helpful in the department. I know in the past some students complained about jealousy between current employees and future students. Some of the staff refused to fully train students for fear it would ultimately put their jobs at risk. Ultrasound techs understood once the student graduated, they would be willing to work for less pay because of their lack of experience. What they failed to realize was no one could take their place. Effective departments kept a mixture of seasoned and fresh employees because each brought different strengths to the table.

I didn't feel any of that energy at the county hospital. I shadowed a guy named Vince who made it clear that I was my only competition. He was assigned to students because he wasn't selfish with information, and he was as patient as a driver's education teacher. Vince confessed how he didn't get proficient or confident at ultrasound until after he graduated and had worked at the hospital for over six months. The vibe seemed to be one of collaboration and I was finally grateful Miss Coleman placed me here.

The next three weeks flew by in a blur. All I did was study ultrasound and show up to work at clinicals. I officially had no time for a personal life. My parents threatened to make a visit to ENEP if I didn't return their calls. I sure as hell didn't want that, so I had my little brother vouch for me. He told them I was fine and just busy with school.

While I was blessed and much more fortunate than some of the other students to have help, I found the support my family extended felt suffocating. What I needed was space to figure things out on my own. I craved the opportunity to hear my own inner voice instead of my parents. That's what I went away to college for. To figure out how to navigate life independent of my original family unit. They seemed to respect my desire for distance but insisted that coming home for breaks and holidays was nonnegotiable.

I let out a sigh of relief. It was my last shift before the weekend, and I was on my way out the door.

"It's a testicle," Vince said with a small grin.

I dropped my belongings and snatched the ultrasound order from his hands. By far, the most surprising thing I learned about the job of an ultrasound tech was that we scan men's balls. For the first week, I skipped all the testicle exams because I thought only men performed those. When Vince told me I couldn't graduate until I was competent in all exams, including testicles, I'd been on the lookout for them ever since.

The department found it hilarious that I eagerly awaited balls every day that I came to train. But that was the type of student I was. I needed to master everything. Vince told me on my first day that every ultrasound tech had an exam they avoided. His advice was to go and do the exams that scared me most. Balls scared the shit out of me.

"Do you need any back up? Or can I start this other exam?" Vince asked although he was already halfway out of the door. Within a week, he allowed me to prepare the patient and start his exams. He would come in after twenty minutes and see if I needed him to finish or if I was able to handle it on my own. After three short weeks, I worked independently. He simply needed to check my ultrasound pictures before they were sent to the radiologist.

"I'm good. I gotta learn them eventually, right?"

"Correct. That's why I like you, Sade. Do the ones that scare you!"

There was a security guard outside of the exam room door. *An inmate?* My heart dropped to my ass. The officer read a magazine like it was 1997. He didn't bother to look up at me.

"What are you supposed to be?" he asked with little inflection in his tone.

"I'm the ultrasound tech. I'm here to perform the exam."

That caught his attention. He made eye contact with me and scoffed. "I don't think so, *Akesha Murray.*"

I blinked several times because I did not expect a fifty-something-year-old white man to know who Akesha Murray was. She was a breathtaking, chocolate, plus-size supermodel. I took the comparison as a compliment.

"Okay, I'm a student. But I'm good and I'm here to do my job. Unless he's a serial rapist or a murderer, I'll be fine."

"I can't discuss what the inmate did. But I'll be right here if you need anything." He returned to his magazine. As I grabbed the door, he added, "He's not a rapist."

"Shit!" *He said not a rapist, but he didn't say not a murderer. That means he killed someone!*

He was laid back on the stretcher with his wrists and legs shackled to the guardrails. But even from the door, I could see he was gorgeous. I hadn't realized that a man could be this beautiful. What in the prison bae? Ironic that the man was in for murder, and he was as sexy as the infamous social media prisoner turned model.

"My name is..." I started to introduce myself but stopped. No matter how fine he was, he was an inmate who didn't need my name for me to do my job effectively. "I'm here to do your exam. How long have you been having pain?"

He regarded me intensely. His light brown eyes burned a hole right through me. *Shit.* I would be forced to do his exam with wet panties.

"I need a guy for this." He spoke for the first time, and it was a struggle for me to concentrate. He had a tattoo of a pair of red lips on his neck, along with a myriad of others. He was a breathing work of art.

"I'll keep it professional. I'm fast, and if you tell me what I need to know I can be done in less than twenty minutes."

He seemed to consider my proposition.

"For about three days."

"What were you doing when the pain started?"

"I just woke up and my nuts hurt."

"Is it constant, or does it come and go?"

"Honestly, I'm trying to let you do your job but you're too fucking pretty. It's hard for me to think straight," he said with a youthful grin on his handsome face.

He wasn't much older than me. I'd seen that he was twenty-five in his chart before I realized he was an inmate. A murderer. I'd forgotten that fact again, but the realization broke the spell I was in.

"Let's just get started. I'm going to cover your penis during the exam. The doctors are only interested in pictures of your testicles. It might be slightly uncomfortable because you're in pain, but what I need to do shouldn't hurt."

I grabbed the gel bottle and placed it on the ultrasound camera.

He laughed loudly.

"What?"

"You gotta be fucking kidding? I'm either incredibly lucky or I'm about to be karmically punished. Because it looks like you're preparing to rub some KY-type jelly on my nuts."

I blushed at his observation. I was a professional in training which made the steps for the exam much more sterile. From a man's perspective, I understood why he said what he did.

"In order for the ultrasound camera to take the picture, I have to use this as a medium. There's an entire physics class on it. I would tell you more, but I hate that class."

He bobbed his head in understanding.

"I get that. But you looking as thick as Charmin, and you smell good enough to eat. Do you have any idea how long it's been since I touched a woman? How long it's been since a woman touched me?"

"Uhhh."

He stared at my county-issued name tag.

"You might wanna get a guy, Sade." He turned his gaze away from me and mumbled, "Sexy ass woman with a sexy ass name."

"OK, good. We got it out of the way. We're both sexy."

"We, huh?" he teased.

I did my best to keep a straight face. I had no business flirting with him.

"It's taking everything you got not to smile at me. Let me have it, I know it's probably heart-stopping and stiff dick-inducing!" At his chosen adjectives, I smiled. "Got damn. That face and those lips should be against the law. Please put it away and get me out of here."

After a few more laughs, I did the exam, and Trey was on his best behavior. It was what he asked me to call him because he cringed when I referred to him by his first name, Booker, listed in the chart. He was the third Booker in his lineage, which was why he preferred to be called by the nickname Trey instead. He said he was close with his dad but wanted some individuality plus he said he grew tired of the long dialogue about the nature of his name. He said it bugged the shit out of him when people said he didn't look like a Booker.

I thought having the same name as Booker T. Washington was dope. He smiled when I said that and I swear my panties were soaked, again. He was so damn sexy. At one point, his eyes drifted to the ceiling. I looked over to see if he was in pain. Male patients often had a difficult time admitting when what I did during the ultrasound caused them discomfort.

It took me less than a second to realize he was not in pain, he was aroused. And holy hell, his dick. I'm not one to be impressed by talks of the size of a man's penis. I felt violated the few times I was sent dick pics no matter what they looked like. But this man's penis was a work of art.

It was long and thick. It was the type of dick I'm sure I'd enjoy riding into multiple orgasms. I caught a glimpse of the side of it when I had to move his gown to prep him for the ultrasound. The testicle exam required me to cover his manhood with a towel. The towel was not nearly large enough when he was aroused. He was tall with big hands and bigger feet, so I guess I shouldn't have been too surprised.

I cleared my throat and turned my head back to my screen. I sat in a puddle of arousal and would need to change my scrubs if I didn't focus on the exam. Trey was quiet. He winced only when I'd done his right side. He had a hernia, but I couldn't tell him. It wasn't my job.

Patients tried to get me to disclose what I saw. They wanted to know whether they needed surgery or if they had cancer. But as an ultrasound tech and a student, I could be fired for any discussion about what I saw. Results fell under the doctor's job description and were considered a diagnosis—I didn't have the credentials to diagnose.

We continued our innocent banner about nothing in particular. My brain said I shouldn't speak to him about anything unessential for the exam, but my gut said otherwise. He was a human and a little decency wouldn't hurt anyone. I had a bad track record with men who didn't deserve my trust. I picked the ones who everyone else thought were good, but behind closed doors they were horrible.

Trey would be labeled a bad person because of what he'd done, but when I was in his presence, I felt like he'd hurt himself before he would hurt me. I'd never had that with an ex. They were all okay until I challenged them or stepped out of line. In retrospect, I had no idea what those closeted controllers were capable of. I hadn't known Trey for more than an hour, and I felt completely comfortable.

"Everything good?" Vince asked as he opened the door to check on me.

"Yep." I stood up quickly like I'd done something I didn't have any business doing. I guess fantasizing about riding this man's face and penis probably was inappropriate, but I immediately figured my thoughts were harmless.

"Sade, it was an absolute pleasure meeting you. Good luck with school and ultrasounding ballsacks."

We both laughed but Vince did not. His jaw was clenched, and he was unamused.

I walked to the door and on the way out responded, "Good luck to you too, Trey. Stay safe."

4

T rey

I'D BEEN WITH BEAUTIFUL WOMEN BEFORE, BUT IT WAS LIKE I couldn't remember their faces or their pussies once I'd seen and smelled Sade. I could smell her the moment she got wet. She thought I hadn't realized but I did. Then I noticed her shift in her seat, which confirmed my suspicions. I had made her wet.

I felt like a horny teenager when I couldn't hide my erection, but her body had betrayed her too when she sat drenched and her arousal floated into my nostrils. Sade was fine and sweet. But most importantly, she treated me like a human. That hadn't happened since I got locked up. She might have been slightly apprehensive, but she wasn't afraid of me either.

The few female guards and counselors I'd come in contact with were shaken when they were near me, even with my hands and feet in handcuffs. The way her eyes drifted to them every now and again when I attempted to get comfortable, made me believe she wanted to ask for them to be taken off me. I was uncomfortable in the cuffs because the fucking guard chose to connect me to the bed in the wrong position.

She had no business working in the county hospital scanning ballsacks. When I got out, the first thing I would do was get her a job that didn't involve an ultrasound exam on a low life; especially not on their balls. Other men didn't operate like me. They most definitely would have taken advantage of her and the situation. I got pissed at the mere thought of someone else in her space. I wondered if she had a man. He obviously wasn't hitting it right if her pussy responded to me the way it did. Once she was mine, her pussy would hibernate in my absence.

I had two months left and the heat was turned all the way up here. Something happened when an inmate was about to be released. It was a mixture of jealousy and hatred that drove the other inmates to test anyone on their way out more than ever. I was almost done, and I wouldn't risk getting into more trouble. But when Joseph's toxic ass snatched up the picture I sketched of Sade, I lost it.

I drew her easily because I memorized every aspect of her cocoa-colored round face. Her thick natural hair with that bun in the front and the back out like half an afro. Her skin was brown like the original hickory syrup. I had never dated anyone as dark or as thick as her. I had a type in the past, but that was instantly replaced when I saw her.

All it took was a slick comment to barely leave Joseph's lips before my knuckles connected with his left temple.

"This is better than porn. And these lips... I'm gon' have fun with this bitc—"

He didn't finish. I punched his ass and he fell asleep like I was a magician with the go word. I grabbed the picture and stuffed it into my briefs.

"Guard!" I yelled, as I lay face down and put my arms behind my back.

He took his time to make his way over to our area. With one look at Joseph knocked unconscious, he sighed and cuffed me.

I got five days of restrictive housing when I put Joseph's ass to sleep. It was worth it. I spent most of it accompanied by thoughts of Sade. I had uninterrupted time to think of how she'd feel in my arms. I thought about where I'd take her out. I dreamed about what our kids would look like if I was lucky enough to shoot the club up.

I wondered if I'd have to wait for her to drop her man if she had one. I considered the likelihood of what I'd do when I saw her again. Would I have to go up to the county hospital like a stalker just to see her? Maybe I'd leave it to that fate shit. I could try to hang back and allow space for the Kismet vibe energy those girl porn books—posing as romance novels—described. I admit I'd enjoyed quite a few of them because I had nowhere else to be.

I recited a poem to myself constantly. It was one of those slam poetry-type pieces and it moved me. I saw it on somebody named Folasade's social media. The account didn't have personal pictures, just poetry and art. The poem invaded my mind now because it made me think of Sade. Everything made me think of her.

All I need is a pen and a pad. If a pen and a pad was all that I had,
then life would still make sense to me.
Symbolically, I paint this pretty little picture of me but in all actuality,
you have no idea what's inside of me, inspiring me.
I been waitin' a long time to speak.
Afraid to be the real me
Scary Sherry is what they used to call me
Now I growl when I speak, grit my teeth when I sleep
Cause I'm the coldest and illest female lyricist you'll eva meet.
I identify with all the lies of the many guys that came in my life...
With no intentions on makin' me they wife.
It hurts me to see girls be the opposite of what we should be
Have Mercy
cause it seems that the bad girls get good men

And bad boys hurt good women
Those doing right live a short life
Women trying to live right can't make life, get it?
Married women can't have kids, wild teens have 'em by the dozen,
Doesn't seem fair, does it?
We got our eyes wide shut cause we blinded by the darkness,
Married to ourselves, wondering where the spark is.
We headed back to our future to end a new revolution
We lookin' to the dead folks for a current solution.
I'm as light as a rock
Loud as a whisper
The heat from my speech will make a grown man shiver
Pay attention, 'cause I make no extensions
I got an assignment for you and it's due last weekend.
When I'm finished with you, I might proclaim it is done,
I know I'm not God but I'm tight with his Son
My life is clear as mud something you can barely see through,
I leave them all wantin' more then tell them look out for the sequel.

. . .

I DIDN'T KNOW WHETHER TO BE INSPIRED OR TURNED ON BY THE artist. She talked big shit and I felt it on a soul level. The first thing I would do when I saw Sade again was ask if her full name was Folasade and if she had ever shared poetry online.

5

Sade

I can't sing but, in my car, and in my mind, I'm an eclectic mixture of Beyoncé and Ariana Grande—can't nobody tell me nothing. I was at a stoplight in the midst of the most tone-death performance of my life when a car from the left lane entered the intersection ahead of me, despite the red light. Stunned at this random and quite dangerous decision, I turned to my left. Did anybody else see this foolishness? The driver was also stunned. He looked at me and shrugged his shoulders as if to say, 'The hell was that?' *It was him.*

"Trey?"

He grabbed his heart like he couldn't be happier to see me. For him to be so hard-bodied and muscular, his actions toward me felt as gentle as a summer's breeze. People honked because he was supposed to proceed forward at his now green turning light. Instead, Big Trey put his truck in park and hopped out like he wasn't in the way of heavy traffic.

He strolled over to me unbothered by the current circumstances. His stroll was confident and sexy. I was sure his big dick rested down by his knees by the way he carried himself. *Lordt, have mercy.* He wore jeans and a simple white T-shirt. They were both sprinkled with what appeared to be oil smudges like he'd been at work.

"Sade," Trey said in an ungodly tantalizing voice. There went my fucking panties.

"Booker Avery Edmund."

His initials spelled bae. It had to be a sign.

Trey dropped his head. "Normally, I don't allow anyone to call me by my government name, but hearing it on your lips..." He grabbed his heart again. "I've never heard anything sexier."

The cars laid on their horns, but Trey didn't break his gaze from mine. "Drive over to that bookstore and meet me by the cappuccino machine," he said with an unrushed wink.

"Viola's?"

"That's the one. I love it there."

Traffic was anxious and I didn't want to hold it up any longer. His satisfied grin made my nipples harden. The smile on his handsome face faltered momentarily as he took in my body's response to him through my thin shirt.

"You're gonna kill me," he said again. "You're so damn pretty."

I berated myself as I pulled out of traffic and parked my car. I had no business at Viola's with a former patient from the county hospital. He had obviously been convicted of murder. What if he murdered young thick dummies who met him at bookstores without even googling him first? *Ugh, I have his entire government name and didn't think to Google him.* Maybe that meant he had nothing to hide.

I grabbed my cell phone and snapped a picture of his truck with the license plate in the frame. I got a blurry picture of him also and texted them both to my little brother.

Me: *Having coffee with a stranger. Call me in an hour.*

Fela: *Where u at?*

Me: *Viola's*

Fela: *Don't make me have to fuck his old ass up! Text me if you need me.*

Me: *Thanks*

Fela: *If you don't pick up when I call, I'm pullin' up.*

Me: *okay*

He was out of his car and headed in my direction, so I wouldn't have much time to look. But curiosity got the best of me. I had to see if there were any links with his name and the nature of his charges. I was so caught up in the headline that I hadn't realized he made it to my side of the car. I screamed when he tapped lightly on the window. The article was entitled, "College Scholarship Recipient's Future Ruined After Conviction of Brutal Murder of Cousin."

"You ready, beautiful?"

I nodded as the words brutal and murder bounced around in my head. He didn't read violent to me. If I was honest with myself, he did seem capable of murder if someone harmed someone close to him. But the person who was killed was his family member. I couldn't think of a valid reason to kill someone related to me.

My problem was I didn't trust my own voice. Society said this man was dangerous, but he didn't feel like a threat to me. Guys from my past were perfect on paper but treated me like they owned me. It wasn't safe to be with those types of men. My gut told me they were the ones who were violent and aggressive.

I got out of my car, and he guided me into the bookstore with his hand resting on the small of my back. It felt intimate without crowding my space. I liked it. And despite the Google information I'd stumbled across, I still wasn't afraid of him. Viola's was a small Black-owned bookstore that featured local and indie authors. There were always scheduled events on the calendar to encourage support for the store and the authors. I agreed to accompany him because I loved the historical location and the store's importance in the city.

"I don't drink caffeine," I said once we were in line.

"Let me guess, you're a caffeine-free tea drinker?" he asked with the same smile that just drenched my fresh panties.

My mouth hung wide open. It was my go-to facial expression when I was shocked and impressed.

He closed his eyes briefly, then leaned down to whisper in my ear. "I'm really trying to be on my best behavior here, but you keeping your mouth open like that makes me want to do unspeakable acts to you."

"Like what?" I asked, because what the hell? I was feeling him and there was no way I would bail now.

He dropped his own sexy mouth at the sound of my audacious words. Before he was able to speak, the cashier asked for our orders. He ordered for us both. It felt like I could relax and for once I didn't have to be in control. When I hung out with ENEP guys, they were so nervous that they wanted me to dictate every aspect of our inter-actions.

It was sweet, but I didn't want to fuck sweet. And with my diffi-cult major and demanding clinical schedule, the last thing I wanted to do was make more decisions. I had a bad case of decision fatigue. When I was away from school, I needed to relax my brain. Like this.

"She'll have an African Solstice tea with a coffee cake." Trey ordered for me without making a huge production out of it. The fact that he wasn't overly dramatic, and he hadn't double-checked with me to see if what he had done was okay, was beyond attractive.

"And what are you having, sir?" the cashier asked politely.

"Sade's pussy would be nice, but since that's not on the menu, I'll have a cold brew."

The cashier was much older than us. She had a kind face and though she worked the register, she reminded me of a warm librarian or someone's great-aunt who made homemade ice cream. Her light honey-colored skin turned bright red, but she maintained composure in her face.

"All right then, one lucky lady will have an African Solstice tea with a coffee cake and one ravenous young man will have a cold brew since his lady is not on our menu. Coming right up," she finished with a wink.

We found a seat in the back of the bookstore. The layout was designed like a reading nook. There were bookshelves on either side of us and above our seats. The seats were cushioned and shaped like open hands. Instead of facing each other, the hands were side by side with a small table in front of them.

"Thanks for not running off. I like you, Sade. I also know you googled me. What do you want to know?"

"What do you want to tell?"

"Nothing. I don't want to talk about shit, but how to please you until you beg me to stop."

I tried my best not to fidget, but it wasdifficult when he spoke to me like that.

"I will though," he continued. "For you. I'll tell you whatever you need to know to feel comfortable with me. You afraid of me, Sade?"

"No. Should I be?"

"I think maybe you should. We met when I was locked up and you just read the headline about me. Did you at least let your home-girls know you're here?"

I laughed loudly. With tears in my eyes, I showed him the texts I sent to my brother.

"Good. I'd be worried if you hadn't. Sounds like your little brother is gonna kick my ass if I step out of line." Trey sipped his coffee and my eyes keyed in on his lips when he did. "I been through some shit. Seen a lot of shit too. But I'd rather walk through an Antarctic blizzard with my balls out before I hurt you—physically or otherwise. You can take that to the bank."

I stared at him. I would be the one to fall for a man with a crim-inal record. He said all the right things. I wanted to shift my focus and the conversation, so I asked, "What school was your scholarship for?"

"ENEP, just like you. I coulda been your man in another lifetime."

"You think you'd be as attracted to me if you never lost your freedom?"

His expression turned serious. "The fuck is that supposed to mean?"

"Don't get it twisted. I know I'm fine and I never have an issue with attracting men. Sometimes I wish the thirsty ones would step off. I just mean that I'm sure you have boatloads of classically beautiful women falling all over you. Women that are more your type."

"And what's my type? Since you know everything."

"Well, let's see, you're buff as shit. You're tall, brown-skinned, and walk with that big dick energy. You probably prefer light to caramel-complected women. Women who do Pilates and CrossFit and have the new model body type: slim-thick. Your type probably wears false lashes and flawless makeup, with naturally long, straightened hair."

I sat back satisfied after what I was confident was the read of the century.

"You got me." His face scrunched up like he'd been caught with his hand in the cookie jar.

My God, this man is irresistible.

"Before I got locked up, what you described was exactly what my girlfriend looked like. But I didn't know shit. I had to grow up quickly. I want more than just fine."

"And now you're looking for a serious, sturdy Black woman to cook your meals and financially take care of you?"

"Absolutely not! I wasn't looking for shit. My balls hurt and I ended up having the sexiest woman I've ever seen do some professionally freaky shit with me that resulted in the pain going away. It was like hoodoo magic." He leaned in my direction to stress his point and his proximity had my breath lodged in my throat.

"As far as holding me down, I'm not one of them young beta males at your school who is looking for a surrogate mother. I know the perception of the Black woman as the work mule who can handle everything. Black women are expected to work, bear children, clean house, fuck, suck, and still get discarded for white or white adjacent. The shit makes me sick to my stomach. I'm not perfect by any means. You were right about my type in the past.

"But I know better now. Plus, I got girl cousins. And just like them, you deserve to be taken care of. I didn't let you pay today, and I don't plan on starting." He shifted his body to face me fully and continued. "I'm saying a lot I know. But if you were mine, like really mine, you'd work only if you chose to. I would take care of you. And when you have my babies, you'll decide if and when you were ready to go back to work.

"Sade, you have a beautiful body, baby. You thicker than a Snickers with a pretty ass face to match. From where I'm sitting, you look good enough to be on the cover of somebody's magazine. The truth is your mind and spirit are equally as attractive. I can't tell you the last time I spoke with a woman, or anyone for that matter, who didn't treat me like I was a low life. If today was the last time I saw you, I'd be thankful to have had a conversation with someone who sees me as a human."

I sat and let his words wash over me. If anyone else had said what Trey did, I would have accused them of trying too damn hard, but there was sincerity in every word he spoke.

"Okay, well shit. Thank you. So, am I your type now?" I asked, grinning. There was no need for me to try to match his level of intensity. I decided to keep it light.

"You silly as shit, you know that?" I shrugged. "There's something else that's been bugging me."

"What?"

"Do you write poetry?"

I froze and my eyes got big.

"I randomly came across the one about having our eyes wide shut 'cause we blinded by the darkness."

"I'm so embarrassed. I can't believe you found that. I posted it last year."

"I recited it to myself often."

"Really?"

"Yeah."

"You're not a stalker, are you?"

"No. I thought maybe it was a coincidence that you had a similar name to the person who wrote it."

I believed him. It was cringe that he read my work and wanted to talk about it out loud, but I believed he hadn't tried to find me. My pictures weren't associated with the account.

I'd finished my tea and coffee cake and allowed Trey to walk me to my car. I braced myself for a weird goodbye because a kiss at this point felt forced. Once I was seated in my car, I lowered the window to see what his next move would be.

"Sade?"

"Yeah, Trey?"

"Let me get your number."

I sighed heavily. I didn't have a problem with that. *What's the worst thing that could come of him having my number?*

6

T rey

Me: What you wearing?

Sade: Scrubs silly. I told you I had clinicals today.

Me: Take'em off

Sade: Please stop. I'm not trying to have wet panties and you are not here to do anything about it.

Me: Stop teasing me. I told you I'm trying to get to know you better before I start exploring your body.

Sade: You started it. You just told me to take my clothes off at the county hospital *green face vomit emoji

Me: You right. Let Vince scan them balls.

Sade: Whatever, Booker.

Me: Call me when you walk to your car.

Sade: You're not the boss of me.

Me: I'm about to be the boss of your pussy.

Sade: *water drops and umbrella emoji
Me: *red hot sweaty tongue hanging out emoji
Sade: *Eggplant and red lips emoji
Me: I'm on my way!
Sade: Later skater

She thought I was kidding when I texted that I was on my way. I could tell when she saw me. I knew the exact moment her panties were wet. I smelled it. Vince gave me the 'watch yourself' look and I returned it. Because who the fuck was this dude supposed to be?

"Trey," she said on an inhale. Her pouty lips looked like they belonged around my dick. The thought made my pants tighten. I tried not to be a creep and keep my distance, but I couldn't take it anymore. Her flirting gave me blue balls. I was too old for this shit. I wanted her and I knew she wanted me too.

"Let me borrow you for a second. You got a break coming up?"

"No," Vince interjected like I asked him to step away.

Now that I wasn't on a hospital gurney with my manhood half exposed, I could fully see his face. He wasn't a bad-looking brotha. I wondered if maybe Sade was attracted to him. He was muscular but smaller than me. I put him at about five feet ten—barely taller than Sade, but maybe she was into that.

He was the book-smart, academic type who would treat her right but wouldn't satisfy her if she gave him play-by-play instructions. I shouldn't have been threatened by him, but I guess I was. He knew I was a former convict and probably didn't approve of my association with Sade. But he would have to get over that shit.

"I don't have a break, but I'm off in thirty minutes. Wait for me," she said silkily. She stepped between us and placed her hands on my chest. *Got damn.* I would wait three hours with the energy she sent my way. I forgot Vince was there.

"I can do that. I brought a book."

She leaned up and placed a sweet kiss on my lips. She tried to step back but I held her in place for a few extra moments. I didn't shove my tongue down her throat, but I accepted hers when she slipped it into my mouth. I was faintly aware we were still in public. She let a small moan of appreciation escape her lips and only moved when Vince cleared his throat. I kept my eyes on her fat ass when she turned to finish her shift with ol' boy.

"Text me and I'll come back."

Sade: Ready to take my clothes off?

Me: You play too much!

I was already outside of her department when her text came through. She walked up to me with her designer lunch and backpack. Damn, she was fine.

"What I gotta do to make you my lady?"

She shifted and rested her weight onto one of her thick thighs as she considered my request. Sade glanced around us, then led me to a semi-private area outside of the doors labeled patient entry.

"If you want me to be your lady, I need you to answer three questions first."

"Anything."

"Would you ever lie to me?"

"No."

"Would you ever hurt me?"

"Fuck no!"

"Would you ever do anything that will get you sent back there?"

Her eyes misted and it pissed me off. Somehow, I felt like I'd already hurt her.

"No. Baby, no. I swear. Look, we just met, so I don't know you very well. Not all the details, like how many siblings you have, your birthday, or your favorite food. But I know all the things that matter. You're kind to people like me, even when others aren't. You sure as hell don't scare easily. You live in Southern California, but somehow you still have faith in people.

"You either have a pure heart or you're really in tune with your intuition. You have goals and you're working hard at them. You're professional and funny too. And I'm feeling you, Sade. I promise I won't do shit to mess up what we have or what we about to have if you let me in—that includes going back to prison."

She smirked at me, and I relaxed. I'd never been seen as a man of few words, but I kept most conversations to a minimum. Sade, on the other hand, had me spilling my guts every time I saw her.

"I have one brother. My birthday is December twelfth, and I can eat Thai food any day of the week. Others see me as impulsive, but I consider myself adventurous. I'm rather turned on by men who take charge as long as they don't try to lock me down in a restrictive way. A little playful jealousy like what you have going on with Vince is attractive. Calling the department to check to see if I am where I say I am will have me running like a track star.

"If you're vying for the position of my man, you need to please me. Listen to me without letting me walk all over you. I'll lose respect for you if I always get my way. Take control of the situation without being controlling and lock me down while giving me the illusion of freedom."

I grinned at her. What she described was the prototype. She had me open to the idea of marriage to keep her all to myself. But because I listened to what she said, I knew she wouldn't go for that. Marriage would have to come much later. The fact that I even said the word in my head meant I fucked with her heavy.

"Where do you need to be right now?"

"It depends," she said. She shrugged her round, sexy shoulders. Even in her scrubs, her titties bounced around like she was in lingerie. The butterfly blue color of her scrubs accentuated her umber-colored skin. It took every ounce of restraint I had not to pick her up and take her to my place to have my way with her.

"On what, Sade Adu?"

Her eyes widened.

"That's the singer's name, right? Sade Adu?"

"Yes, but most people don't know that. You surprised me with this one."

"Is Sade your full name or is it Folasade?"

"The latter," she responded with fire in her eyes.

"Folasade. That's beautiful. I didn't know if you signed your poetry that way to be artistic or if it was your given name."

"It's on my birth certificate."

"Where do you need to be?" I asked again, as I stepped closer and invaded her space.

"It depends. Are you still getting to know me? Or are you trying to explore my body?"

I froze. The hood violins started to play music in my head like this was the part of the movie where the guy said something overly affectionate. We weren't in a romantic comedy, and she wasn't the man. But her words sent shock waves to my dick *and* my chest. I grabbed her hand tightly enough where she knew she didn't have a choice, but it was also clear I wouldn't hurt her. She did a half gasp half moan and my dick started head banging.

"You trust me?"

She nodded her sexy head ever so slightly.

"I gotta hear it, baby. You ready for me? I'm not gon' be calling your department looking for you, but I might text you looking for my pussy."

"Your pussy?"

"Yeah, Fola! I just know it's gon' be fire. If I put my face between your thighs, that pussy will belong to me. If you even think about me, she will leak. If you hear my voice, she will pulse. And if I tell you to bring me my pussy, she will come."

"Okay."

"Okay, what?" I asked more forcefully.

"Okay," she said again, challenging me.

She followed me through the parking lot until we arrived near my vehicle. I unlocked my truck and quickly opened the trunk of my luxury SUV. She was sexually adventurous, but I wouldn't touch her until she said yes. Once I was inside of my flatbed, I reached my hand out to pull her up. She just stared at me with a smirk and tucked her juicy lip between her teeth. She arched an eyebrow, then crossed her arms. I took a deep breath because I wasn't into playing games but I also kind of liked this shit with her.

"I'll beg if you make me."

She rolled her eyes but couldn't hide her smile. I jumped down and lifted her over my shoulder. She was extra thick, but when I was locked up, I squatted up to four hundred pounds—Sade was light work. Her soft weight against my shoulder wasn't shit. She was impressed with the way I handled her.

I laid her down gently and put my hands down her panties. They were soaked. And she had the hood of her clit pierced. *Shit!* She was a freak and I had just hit the jackpot.

"Can I explore your body, Folasade?"

I still had my hands down her pants. Her head was thrown back, and her mouth was slightly open. I stopped the movement of my fingers, and her eyes popped open.

"Don't stop, Trey."

"Tell me I can have your body."

She hesitated, so I squeezed her clit between my fingers.

"Mmhm, Trey."

"Call me Booker."

"Booker."

"Yeah, you like that?"

She didn't respond, so I stopped my finger strokes once again.

"Okay." She relented. "Booker Avery Edmund, you can *borrow* my body."

I chuckled because she was stubborn as shit. She'd made it a point to stress that I could borrow and not have her physical form.

"I'm not gonna play with your pussy until you clearly tell me that I can have it."

I removed my hands from her panties and snatched her scrub bottoms down. With no warning, I put my beard up against the juncture of her thighs.

"You smell so damn good. Shit! But I'm not gonna taste you until you tell me I can have you."

She moaned loudly. We weren't close to the hospital, but we were still in the parking lot. I didn't give a fuck.

"You can have my pussy! Explore my body, please, daddy!"

I lost it. Like the blackouts I had when I was upset, I don't remember how long I ate her pussy. I know I've never smelled or tasted a pussy so savory. Sade had a pussy that could make a man orgasm by just looking at it. I could have eaten her jewel until the sun came up. But she said stop. I stilled.

"What's wrong?" she asked, out of breath.

"You said stop." I wouldn't continue after she said stop no matter how freaky the game. I was fresh out of the penitentiary. While I enjoyed this cat-and-mouse shit we played, I had my limits.

"No, I said please stop as in I'm about to lose my fucking mind if you don't let me feel you inside of me. With your dick, Booker, please."

"Oh, okay, we need a safe word. I don't wanna hurt you or have any misunderstandings about what you want."

"No."

"That won't work, baby. You like playin' with me, being challenging and shit. If I'm honest, I like it too. I just gotta know for sure when to stop."

"How about red for stop and yellow for slow down?"

"Yes. Now bring me my pussy."

She pulled her bottoms off the rest of the way and opened her legs wide into the same shape as an extended letter V.

"Damn, you flexible as fuck, Sade. Shit, shit, shit." I gripped her thighs and cursed at my misstep.

"What's wrong?"

"I, uh... I was serious about getting to know you first. And uh, I'm a little out of practice with this shit."

"Spit it out, Booker. My pussy is throbbing."

"Not helping," I said. I released her thick thighs and tried to steady my breath. "I didn't bring protection. They tested us when I was inside, but I can't put you at risk. You're too good for that."

"Damn, thank you for being so considerate, handsome! But I have rubbers with me." Her eyes were almost nonexistent when her round cheeks rose as she smiled. "I've been wanting to fuck since I took them ultrasound pictures of your balls." Sade's sensual stare made me smile like an idiot.

She leaned over to get into her bag, and I saw an unobstructed view of her ass. It was glorious. All the fantasies and wet dreams I'd had about her when I was locked up, paled in comparison to the real thing. I slapped her ass so hard she almost fell face forward. I yanked her back toward me to steady her, then put my face between her ass cheeks and ate her pussy from the back. I saw the rubber under her hand and swiped it to put it on. I entered her drenched center, and my soul was immediately snatched from my body.

"You feel good, Trey," she purred.

I grabbed her natural hair and pulled her chin upward. She was forced to look at me upside down. "The fuck I tell you about calling me Trey?" I gritted out. It was strange how much I hated my government name until she said it.

"Sorry, Treeeeey," she whined again, disobediently.

I picked up the pace and gave her my entire length. I needed to teach her sassy ass a lesson. I fucked her like I wanted to the first time I smelled her scent. I lifted my mustache toward my lip, like the freak I was, and took a deep breath. The smell made me ram my dick into her harder. She moaned and kept her lips closed in defiance like she refused to audibly express her pain.

"Damn, baby. This pussy belong to me?"

"Maybe."

I pulled out of her and turned her over on her back to face me. It was a mistake. Her eyes were filled with lust.

"Is this pussy mine?"

"Maybe." She continued to challenge me.

"Matter of fact, I want you naked. Take all this shit off."

Sade removed her clothes unhurriedly. It pissed me off and

turned me on at the same damn time. Once her clothes were off, I growled, "Take all that shit off too."

"I'm naked, Tre... Booker. What are you talking about?"

"That jewelry shit is sexy, but it's like you still have clothes on. I can't get to your clit like I want. And I intend to attend to your nipples. I'd say the same thing if you had your tongue pierced. I'd want to feel your entire tongue on me, without the ball. Take the gold metal out. Now!"

"Uh, baby?"

"Yeah?"

"I do have my tongue pierced, it's just pink because you can't have facial jewelry in the hospital. And I'm not taking my piercing out in your truck. I'll mess around and get an infection."

"Fine, but next time, I want you in my bed and I want you naked!"

She rolled her eyes at me. She was a little sweet and a lot of fucking heat. *Sweet heat. Hell yeah!*

I pushed her legs back and half expected her to protest, but she didn't. Instead, she hit a happy baby type of pose. I didn't have the mental capacity to figure out if she was double-jointed or if it was wishful thinking. The bottom of my balls tingled, though I didn't plan to cum until she'd had at least one orgasm. I cupped my hands underneath her thick ass cheeks and whispered in her ear.

"You like it, baby?"

"Yes!" she moaned back.

As I slammed into her again, I muttered, "I'm sorry I didn't make the first time special. You probably like rose petals and soft music when you're making love."

"Maybe a little. But I don't want that."

"What chu want?"

"Just you, Booker. Just you."

I flicked her right nipple ring. It was a deluxe gold hoop that was twin to the left one. I bent down and tugged it gently into my mouth. She yelped. I sucked her nipple like the criminal I was. I was locked and loaded. My mission was to make her orgasm so hard that her legs wouldn't work afterward.

Sade pushed her fingernails into my triceps. Her body vibrated from the shockwaves that flowed through her. She came hard. When she opened her eyes, I let her legs down. She wrapped them around me lazily.

"Damn, you're pretty when you cum." I put my attention back on her breasts. "You gonna have this shit out next time, right?"

She didn't respond. So, I flicked her right nipple harder.

"Make me," she said, with that damn smirk on her face.

This girl was like an amusement park. I'd waited to fuck for at least two years. I had sex a few times in the beginning with one of those church ladies who came to do the prison ministry. Shit was foul on my part, but she basically put it in my face. The last time we did it, we got caught and I felt awful. She wasn't married or anything, but she was a good girl—except for when she fucked around with me.

After the prison ministry chick, I told myself I'd wait to have sex until I found someone I liked. I adored Sade. Even though I didn't know her well, I wanted to spend time with her. I had an uncontrollable urge to get to know her and her body better.

Still, she challenged me, and I had to do something about it.

"Turn your thick ass over and take this shit from the back!"

She flipped over on her hands and knees and tooted her ass up at me. She rested her hands against the floor of my truck's trunk.

"Hell nah!" I pushed the center of her back, so the side of her round face rested against the truck where her hands had been. I plunged inside of her firmly. I asked again, "Next time I see you, you're gonna be completely naked, right?" I plunged into her again and made her whimper.

"Yeah," she whined.

"That sexy ass metal shit too?"

"Yes. Yellow."

"Damn, baby, am I hurting you?"

"Yes."

"Want me to stop?"

"No, just slow down."

"Like this?" I slowed down my strokes, but I kept them deep.

"Fuck, yes!"

I rocked in and out of her until sweat beaded on my forehead. That's when I felt her soft, thick hands massage my balls. The balls I wanted her to touch so badly that night at the hospital.

"Oh shit, Sade! I'm 'bout to come, baby."

"You sharin' this dick with anybody else?"

"Man, hell naw! It's yours if you want it, baby."

"Yes! Cum for me, Booker."

My climax was so strong, I was half convinced I'd gotten her pregnant.

7

───────────────

T rey

My place was outside of the city, but Sade liked to stay
close to campus. So here we were. We walked around campus and flirted like some kids. If I was honest, I enjoyed it. We spent time together whenever she wasn't busy with school. My part-time gig was flexible. I helped a neighborhood mechanic until I could plot out my next move.

"I need to talk to you about something," I said and led her to an empty bench between two poorly constructed buildings. It took me a second to focus because I couldn't figure out who the hell made the plans for it.

"What's up? You look like you're gonna be sick."

I stood, although I sat only a few moments before.

"I killed my cousin with my bare hands."

Sade would leave my Black ass the moment she processed the

words I spoke. My eyes were closed because I couldn't stomach it if I saw fear in her expression.

"Booker?"

Her soothing voice and the flutters I got when she said my name caused me to direct my gaze to the bench where she sat. When I did, her hand was outstretched. I took it and reclaimed my seat beside her. I waited several more painstaking moments for her interrogation or judgement, but neither came so I continued.

"I did it because he was hurting another family member."

Sade let me finish and didn't rush the conversation at all. It meant the world to me that she hadn't shown a hint of disdain toward my past, even though I'd been in shackles when we first met. It was important that whatever the hell I had with her wouldn't be ruined because of my decisions. I didn't regret what I did, but because of my feelings for her I was willing to share the whole truth to preserve what I hoped was the beginning of something more permanent.

My head was lowered as I considered how to describe why I did it.

"Sean was... he was—"

Sade used her finger to redirect my attention to her. *Damn, she's beautiful.*

"It doesn't matter."

"I want you to hear it from me. I don't want you to have to use the internet when I could tell you myself."

"The nature of your crime doesn't bother me."

My clenched hands relaxed, and my heart tightened. I was sure I'd experienced romantic love or something close to it. But it was clear to me I'd only been infatuated with the women I knew before I went away. In the short time I'd known Sade, I'd fallen for her body, and I was convinced I would fall for everything that came with it.

"But..."

Fuck! Why is there always a but? I bounced my knee and did my best to be as patient with her as she was with me.

"But what?" I asked.

"But it seems like it bothers you. I'm worried that might affect us down the line."

"What do you mean?" I had no idea what the hell she meant.

"You offered to tell me whatever I wanted to know when we met at Viola's. It was clear you didn't want to talk about it, but you said you would for me. Then you asked if I was scared of you. Nothing has changed on my part. I've never been afraid of you, and I don't need to know what you did."

I got that tingly feeling in my chest and my stomach when she cut to the heart of the situation. She didn't dance around the tough shit. I was most impressed that with all she knew, and all she chose not to know, she wasn't afraid of me.

"I guess we did talk about it the first time we spoke outside of the hospital."

"We did. If you don't lie to me, hurt me, or go back, I'm good."

I considered her words. I was taken aback by the amount of faith she had in me.

"Back to the part about it bothering you. If you don't face whatever it is from your past that made you feel the need to bring it up with me again, I'm afraid it might affect our future."

I leaned in and kissed her on her cheek. "Thank you, baby. I'll keep that in mind."

I appreciated Sade's perspective. However, I had no intention of dwelling on the past. If she was cool with my history of violence, I intended to focus on the present... with her in my life. We continued our walk through campus hand in hand. I'd done a lot of shit for females in my past but kissing and holding hands wasn't one of them. PDA with Sade felt right. I did it for her and for any man who questioned her availability. We didn't need to be official for them to know to steer clear.

There were a couple of guys who were bold enough to walk over and speak to her while I stood there.

"Folasade! What's happening, youngin?" this swole kid asked.

"What the hell?" My eyebrows furrowed. He fit the description of an athlete. Both in the way he was built and carried himself. I guessed he was probably a football player. But my real issue was how familiar he was with my lady.

"Oh, it's not like that. We're all just friends. Nothing more. Not play brothers or play cousins that secretly get down, just friends," his smiling-ass friend said.

"Baby, this is D and his roommate Rashad."

"Oh shit, why you ain't just say that?" I didn't have a problem with gay men. As big as they were, they could be her friends and look out for her.

"Noooooo," Rashad said. He exaggerated the word and grabbed a whimsical-looking chick that could have been a real-life Black fairy. "This is my lady. D's ass is too big for me." He grinned like he didn't have a care in the world.

"You play too fuckin' much, Rashad," D said.

"I'm D. My fianceé is somewhere painting and being antisocial." He gripped me up hard as fuck. Was this fool trying to break my hand? "We met your lady a few weeks ago on campus when she was walking by herself in the dark."

I shifted my gaze to Sade and frowned at her. It wasn't safe for her to walk around campus alone. It didn't matter if the other students were weak to me. They could do serious damage to my lady if they caught her on her own.

"We walked her to her car and told her we had her back if any of the ENEP creeps texted her any more dick pics."

"The fuck?" I turned my whole body to face her.

"It's OK, baby. I'm fine," she insisted. She put her hands on my chest to calm me. I was still pissed at the reality that somebody had the balls to send her pictures of their dick, but now I wanted to take her home.

"Well, I know that look. We'll let you both be on your way," Rashad's lady interjected. "Nice to meet you...?"

"Trey," I said. I took her hand to my lips and nodded my head at the fellas.

Rashad and Sade frowned.

"Excuse me?" Sade asked, as her three friends walked away.

"Dick pics?" I shot back. "Bring your thick ass over here so I can play with your booty."

She rolled her eyes but did as I said. Damn, I fucked with this girl heavy. I was quite relieved to know there were some real ones who looked out for her while she was on campus.

<hr>

A FEW WEEKS AFTER I TRIED TO TELL SADE ABOUT SEAN, I MET her younger brother, Fela. No one in the family was Nigerian but they unquestionably loved their musical artists. He was silent for half the time I was at their parents' home until I called him Fela Kuti. His eyes lit up, though he tried to hide it.

"What's your favorite Fela song?"

Without hesitation, I responded, "Lady".

"What you know about 'Lady'?"

"She gon' saaaaaay I be lady oh."

Fela laughed and finally loosened up. I wasn't sure what she'd told her family about me, but I figured she hadn't told them everything. They were all open, apart from the expected 'What are your plans with our Sade' questions. I'm good with people and I'm honest. If the subject of my conviction ever came up—which at some point it inevitably would—I'd tell the truth.

Things went left when I took her to meet my family the following week. I have the typical hood adjacent family. My dad wouldn't put clothes on, so he wore his robe and had an unlit cigarette dangling from his lips the entire time. He told me Sade had a hell of a backside in a rather uncouth tone. Her freaky ass giggled when she overheard him.

She was engaged in a relaxed conversation with my hugging Aunt Nae. She's the aunt who made everyone part of the family before she knew them well. If Aunt Nae didn't like somebody, she talked trash about them to the entire city. So far, she seemed impressed with Sade. Aunt Nae said something about fire signs needed to stick together. When Sade responded, 'Or blow this shit to the ground!' My auntie nearly had a laughing stroke.

"You sure you can keep up with her, Trey?" Aunt Nae asked loud enough for everyone to hear.

"I do okay," I responded and winked at my lady.

"Aww hell. Your Aunt Fae is here," Aunt Nae announced with a sad sigh. She was the one who thought I deserved more time.

Aunt Fae was my Aunt Nae's twin sister. They were as different as night and day. If there was only room in the womb for one kind twin, that twin would be my Aunt Nae. My Aunt Fae was mean-spirited. Most people were surprised to learn that they grew up in the same household. My mom was the only one who could level with her sister, Fae.

My mom was the oldest, so even though her little sister was wicked, Aunt Fae respected her. If I'd known she would stop by, I wouldn't have come. I sure as hell wouldn't have brought Sade.

"Look what the devil dragged in," Aunt Fae said before she was fully in the house. Her beady eyes peered into my soul. I stared back but said nothing. I didn't give a shit. Her ways didn't scare me. She was more of an inconvenience. I avoided her simply because I didn't need the distraction. I only entertained people, places, and things that encouraged my growth and peace.

When my aunt walked into the living area, she literally smelled vile.

"Who invited this thug to my sister's house?"

"Is your aunt calling you a thug?" Sade asked and stood up from her seat. If I wasn't so on guard, I would have been turned on. She was prepared to step to my nutty aunt for me. Now I had to make her my non-suffocated wifey.

"And who is this fat bitch supposed to be?"

My Aunt Nae jumped in her sister's face. "That's enough! This is your nephew."

"Sean was your nephew!" she yelled, effectively silencing the entire house.

"Dad, Momma, we're going to head out!" I said and grabbed Sade by her waist. What I wouldn't do was argue about Sean's psychotic ass. On the way to the door, Chris shoulder-checked me. I fell back and bumped into Sade. My chest heaved up and down as I turned to check on her.

"You good?"

"Yeah, let's go so I can put my mouth on your eggplant," she whispered to me. I grinned at her. She made me smile during one of the most stressful situations I'd been in since I got out.

"No!" Chris clapped. He yelled so loudly it startled us both. "You will not play house after you killed my brother!" He ran toward me at full speed. I shoved Sade out of the way and held my hands up in surrender.

"I'm not trying to fight you, man."

"You think I give a *fuck* what you trying to do?" He had tears in his eyes. "I knew Sean didn't fuck with you like that, but what could he possibly have done for you to kill him!"

"I'm not going to be the one to tell you that. Everybody in here knows what happened. Some of them might be in denial, but they all know. Ask your mom what Sean was doing when I came over that day. Let it come from her."

"I want you to tell me!" he screamed.

"Let's go, baby." Sade grabbed my hand and turned toward the door.

But her efforts were halted when Chris yanked her by the neck of her shirt. I blacked out.

"Muthafucker, are you crazy?" I picked him up over my head and dropped him to the ground. I straddled him and punched him with my left and right, repeatedly. My aunts yelled and my dad tried to pull me off, but I wouldn't stop. I couldn't. He snatched my lady, and it flipped on a switch that had been dormant for years.

"Baby, your aunt is calling the police."

I heard Sade's distant voice like my head was underwater. My arms were tired, and when I looked at my knuckles, they were bloody. I gazed up at Sade and for the first time, she looked afraid of me. I stood.

Chris was crying, but it wasn't because of the physical pain. Maybe he didn't really want to fight. Maybe this was simply his way of processing his grief. I missed Sean too. At the same time, what he did was unforgivable. I was right then, but maybe I was wrong this time.

Chris didn't pose a legitimate threat to my woman. He acted like an ass, but I could have corrected him with words. I knew this. I had misused my training and scared the girl of my dreams. He needed to know the truth about Sean, but it wasn't my place.

8

S ade

I WOULDN'T RESPOND TO BOOKER'S MESSAGES. I HAD BEEN IN love only once before and I was sure my heart was headed in that direction with him. That was precisely the reason I couldn't go any further. He would break my heart. I loved how he cared for me in the little time we'd spent together. I wasn't well versed on soul mates, but time didn't have a bearing on how protective he was with me in the same way he was with the other people who meant the most to him in his life. I was confident that was what he'd been doing even if he didn't use words to say it. I had a place in Booker's heart.

I loved how he handled me sexually. I don't think I could call our sex lovemaking, yet no matter how risqué we were, it felt more than a physical act. It turned out, I appreciated how territorial he was with me. It made me feel safe as opposed to suffocated like it did with my exes.

But his protective side easily morphed into violence. That violence, no matter how righteous, would get him sent back to prison. And that was 'Red' for me. I refused to date him while he was locked up—It was a hard limit. So, I needed to protect my heart. I cried myself to sleep each night.

He still sent his evening and morning texts, and I relished the fact that he didn't go overboard since I hadn't responded. He gave me space without letting me drift too far.

Last night, *B.A.E: Beautiful, you made it home safely. I know this because I asked D to stalk you a little. When I did, he laughed and asked if I was fuckin' up. I ain't want to, but I told him the truth.*

This morning, *B.A.E: D told me you looked like you been crying all night. Let me make it better. How can I make it up to you?*

This afternoon, *B.A.E: I miss you.*

Me: typing bubble, typing bubble, typing bubble. Erase.

I was a mess at clinicals. Vince asked if I wanted to take the rest of the day off. I insisted work was a good distraction, so he dropped it. I was grateful for that. If I had to speak about Booker, I probably would have burst into tears. This from a girl who routinely made fun of my friends who cried over a guy. My heart was broken.

TREY

MY HEAD WAS FUCKED UP NOW THAT SADE WOULDN'T TAKE MY calls. I was perpetually pissed and worried I'd end up mixed up in something that would get me sent back. Gabe called. His timing was impeccable.

"Hello, this is a collect call from Gabe Johnson, an inmate at the Norema Correctional Facility. Will you accept the charges?"

"Yes."

"What's up, nephew?" Gabe asked. He sounded as wise and

peaceful as I remembered. Gabe became my mentor when I was inside. He was the one who recommended I choose wisely between the options to read books or lift weights to run the clock out. For Gabe, idle time was not an option. He was in low-level security when I met him, but he'd gotten moved to medium once some additional gang-related charges were brought against him.

"Not too much," I responded unenthusiastically.

"Uh oh. I know woman troubles when I hear them. You know I have five boys?"

"Nah, you never mentioned it before."

"I don't share too much about my family situation with other inmates. But you've become more than just a fellow convict. You're like a nephew. So, tell me what's on your mind, Trey."

"I met someone."

"Is she fine?"

"The finest. You know that chick, Akesha Murray?"

"The plus-sized model who did Beyoncé's clothes?"

"That's the one. My lady could be her sister. Hickory skin, round hips, and lips to match."

"You lucky son of a bitch! No disrespect to Miss Lola."

We laughed a bit longer until silence stretched between us.

"You fucked up?"

"Yeah. Well, not exactly. I got into a fight with Sean's brother."

"Fweeer." Gabe whistled in understanding.

"She was there," I started. "Chris wanted to know what Sean did that would trigger me to the point of killing him."

"You tell him?"

"Nah. It shouldn't come from me."

"What's this got to do with Akesha?"

"Sade."

"No shit? That's a sexy ass name."

"She was there."

"How bad did you fuck him up, Trey?"

"She was telling me that we should leave my folk's house because

Chris was verbally escalating. We were on our way to the door when he grabbed her by the neck of her shirt. I know she wasn't technically in danger. Nevertheless, my body took over like she was. Jamie was in danger. That's a fact. Sade wasn't.

"Now she won't take my calls. I know she's getting my texts. Sometimes she will start to text me back, but she erases it at the last minute. I can see the bubbles appear and disappear on my phone before you even ask." I teased his old ass because he didn't know shit about technology.

"Sade is a genuine girl. She's fiery, but still pure in her spirit. She has never been afraid of me, but since I beat Chris's ass in front of her, she's scared I'll end up back inside. That's a hard line for her. If I'm honest, I'm terrified I'll get thrown back in with these blackouts. The only reason I snapped out of it was hearing her say my aunt was calling the police. What do I do, Gabe?"

"Go back to where it all started."

"To Sean?"

"Well, yes. But before that, I suggest you return to the academy. Gotta go, nephew!"

"I spent your whole time talking about my problems."

"Helps me as much as it helps you. I love you, Trey. You have every answer to any question you'll ever have, inside of you already."

"Stay up, G."

The line disconnected. I texted my dad right away. He was the one who found the professor who trained me after my first blackout.

Professor Sebastian served fifteen years in the Marine Corps. The racism he endured when he grew up in the South, and later while he was in the military, fueled his temper. That temper was responsible for his year-long sentence in the only maximum-security prison in the United States. He had the same condition of righteous anger that I had.

He'd be the one to later teach me that nobody cares if the anger is righteous. If there was violence involved, consequences would come. He broke the face of a captain in the Marine Corps who grabbed the breast of his date at the military ball. He says he never wanted to go, but that the Marine Corps ball was mandatory.

His date divulged her sexual abuse history early in their relationship. Professor Sebastian revealed it was this information along with the fact that they were two of five Black people in attendance that sent him into an activated state. His activated state mirrored my blackout experiences. He physically assaulted a white superior officer in the presence of an all-white service branch that didn't want him there anyway. The ones who did could not excuse blatant violence between an enlisted soldier and an officer. Professor Sebastian was a Master Sergeant before the incident.

After his year at Leavenworth, he was dishonorably discharged and suicidal. He said he made a plan to end his life, but the night before he was to go through with it, he had the most lifelike dream he'd ever experienced. In this dream, he had a conversation with his ancestors. This dream didn't include his grandmother or grandfather, but these family members were with his distant relatives.

Professor Sebastian said he didn't have any practical evidence the people from his dream were actually related to him, but he had a strong gut feeling about who they were. He said they spoke in Bantu language which he later learned was Bube. They spoke to him in Bube, but he heard them in English. Their message for him was that it was not his time yet.

When he asked who they were, they said, 'We are your people. You are our son. And your work is incomplete.' They referred to him as Bojiammo. Through his research, the professor learned that the word was used to refer to a priest. He recounted the dream to me in detail.

"I'm a disgrace to myself. I have no idea how to control myself. I thought I was protecting her, but I ended up ruining my life. I'm a danger to others. The best thing I can do is be done with living. There's gotta be something better than this."

"There is, Bojiammo, but only when your assignment is complete. Your pain is real, but it is temporary. You must learn to transmute

your energy. Use your pain and your testimony to set other Black men free. We remain enslaved. Not merely in the physical body, but most importantly in our mentality. Trust that your gift will make room for you."

"This sounds good, but I have nothing. No plan and no money. I joined the Marines because I couldn't afford to go to college, and I surely couldn't remain at home. I don't have any financial support. No disrespect, but I don't need a sermon, I need a plan."

"As you wish!"

When the professor awoke from the dream, his phone rang. It was his uncle. His uncle said he had a dream that he needed to take Professor Sebastian to an unknown address, or they would both die. He took him to a gym about twenty minutes from his house. Neither of them had ever been there.

Professor Sebastian started to train that day and claimed his life has been blessed and nonviolent ever since. It would be several years later that his ancestry with the Bubi people from the Bioko Island would be revealed.

Professor Sebastian was older than my dad, but he looked my age. He sat at the park involved in an intense game of chess with a ten-year-old kid. I watched from the side as the kid put my professor in check.

"Checkmate," the kid said quietly. He didn't look emotional about the win at all. In fact, he seemed like the outcome was exactly what he predicted.

"Good game, Professor," Professor Sebastian told the kid who wore glasses and had a mouth full of braces.

"You didn't do too bad yourself, Sebastian," he replied.

Professor Sebastian bowed to the prodigy and walked toward my bench. I wasn't ready to face him. I hadn't seen him since before my conviction.

"Why didn't you call me before you went away?" He sat a few feet away from me on the same bench but faced the lake.

I swiped a single tear from my face. I couldn't bring myself to speak about my dishonorable behavior, so I didn't address his question.

"I'm in trouble again."

"Did you take another soul?"

"No. Not yet. It's the blackouts. They're back." I cleared my throat before I continued. "Sean, the soul I took, I kicked his brother's ass... I assaulted his brother."

"What did he do that you felt it was necessary to use physical force?"

"He yanked my lady by the collar of her shirt. I lost time again."

"See you at five," he said and stood.

"Professor, you can't mean tomorrow morning?" I was unprepared for the level of training I knew was to come.

He faced me for the first time. "Do you want to live?"

"Yeah..."

"See you at five."

9

———————

Trey

I could barely walk after another session at the academy. The most ironic aspect of my new training was that I still hadn't set foot on the mat. It had been two weeks of grueling work in the gym but off the mat. Professor Sebastian said I hadn't proved I was worthy to train on his mat. Instead, I'd done every type of cleaning and maintenance in and around the building. I did it without question.

Shit, I wanted to live... And I wanted my lady back. When the professor spoke to me about non-academy topics, it seemed it was always in riddles. He asked me what I knew and when was the last time I listened to myself. I had no idea what he meant and thought most of what he said had gone in one ear and out the other. My 'why' was so strong I would have washed his car to stay out of prison.

I found myself en route to see Chris. I had no got damn business anywhere near that place, but I believe it was my inner self who told me to go. Chris didn't stay with my aunt anymore. She was so broke she didn't have the money to move—she still lived in the house where it happened. But Chris's place was in a nearby neighborhood.

My stomach was in knots at the thought of the ghosts from my past. Although I still felt I shouldn't be the one to tell Chris what happened that night, I couldn't continue to watch him suffer because of his ignorance. I parked my car on the street and wandered up the driveway. I was sore as fuck from all the physical tasks at the academy.

Chris met me on his porch with a pistol in his hand. I froze. If I died today, I would accept my Karma. I wasn't ready to go, but I understood it wasn't up to me. Chris's face was blue and mangled. He still had tape across his nose, which was likely broken.

"You got some fuckin' nerve."

I had my hands in front of me. "I'm just here to tell you the truth." Chris lowered the pistol, but he didn't put it away. "Can I come closer?"

He nodded with hesitation. His eyes searched mine to see if I'd come on some bullshit, but Chris knew I wasn't a liar. I was a lot of things, but in the time we'd grown up, I never lied.

He tucked his strap in his waistband and took a seat on the top step that led to his porch. I approached him and stood off to the side.

"I don't know where to start."

"How about from the beginning?" His voice was rough. Normally, I would have responded with my hands, but that seemed unnecessary. I could see the bigger picture now. My hands allowed me to avoid tough conversations and most of all vulnerability.

"I apologize for hitting you."

His hand went to his waistband. "What happened with my brother?"

"Me and Sean never got along. Since we was kids, it was always me and you."

"Sean was crazy. We all knew it, but he was family."

"It was more than that. I didn't trust him. I felt like something was off with him. It was different. I mean shit, I'm crazy too."

Chris laughed, and it caught me off guard. When I smiled, he frowned.

"Get to the point."

"I'm trying, man. The last thing I want is to ruin your memory of your brother."

Chris gazed into the street as if he hadn't considered that. "I hear you, but you owe me this."

"You can't unknow this shit. What I saw still haunts me."

Chris peered up at me. He was scared, but he wouldn't rest until he knew.

"Jamie..." My voice faltered. I felt the beginning of a blackout, but I continued. "You remember Jamie?"

"Of course. Our cousin. She used to stay at our house when Aunt Wendy was at work. She moved and never looked back."

I cleared my throat. I wanted to check on Jamie, but Gabe and Professor Sebastian thought it was a bad idea. They both believed I should let her come to me if and when she was ready.

"Sean spent a lot of time with Jamie."

"So, what? We all did."

"Yeah, but he lied on me to her and started trying to pit her against the rest of the cousins."

"Trey, I'm trying to follow this shit, but you ain't makin' no sense. We cousins. We all hung out. Boy girl shit didn't matter yet."

"Age did. He was nineteen and she was barely thirteen."

Chris looked like he was in thought over our ages since it had been years. "That sounds about right. But Sean wasn't a knucklehead off the block, he was her cousin."

"When I came over, he was trying to have sex with her."

Chris bolted from his seat and snatched the piece from his pants. "You fuckin' liar."

I put my hands up only to put him at ease. I still wasn't scared. "Am I?"

I could hear his ragged breaths. He was torn between what I'd said and what he wanted to believe about his brother.

"I'm not the only one who knows. I told you to ask your mom. My mom said she caught him with Jamie before when she was much younger. But he came up with some excuse about them playing a game."

"You tryin' to tell me you killed Sean because he raped our cousin?"

"Not that day he didn't."

Chris lowered his weapon. I released a breath proud that I hadn't blacked out. He had a lot of nerve to put a gun to my head. I could have easily disarmed him and killed him with his own damn weapon. But I'd already rearranged his face. I could give him a pass.

"I don't believe you."

I took a seat beside him. "Yeah, you do."

We sat quietly for what felt like an hour—It was likely five minutes.

"Sorry about your girl. She didn't have shit to do with any of this."

"I appreciate that. Like I said, sorry I fucked up your face."

"I shoulda shot your ass," Chris said. He laughed quietly.

"I know it's messed up, but I miss him too."

Chris's body stiffened, then he blew out a tortured breath. "Sean was my brother, and on principle, I should take you out. But if what you said is true…"

He didn't finish his statement, but he didn't have to. I understood his dilemma. Because I was the only kid when I grew up, each of my cousins were like my siblings. I loved them all, just like Chris did.

"Daddy."

I looked toward the door and saw the prettiest little girl version of my cousin. She couldn't have been more than six years old. She was dressed in pink with glitter on her cheeks and in her hair.

"What's up, knucklehead?"

Chris stood and gathered the tiny child in his arms.

"Who is this?"

She pointed her finger in my direction.

"This is your Uncle Trey."

I didn't stay at Chris's house too long after I met his daughter. When he introduced me the way he did, my heart skipped a beat. I couldn't technically be anyone's uncle, but my cousins were basically my siblings. I also think his referral to me as Uncle Trey was his weird way of welcoming me back. After all he'd been through, I'd take it. Now if I could only figure out how to get my girl back, I'd be good to go.

10

S ade

I FELT MORE LIKE MYSELF AGAIN. I MISSED BOOKER DEARLY, but he wasn't worth my mental health. He had anger issues that could get both of us hurt. I uploaded more poetry online and I went back to yoga at the studio instead of on the internet. A month passed since I last spoke to him, and he still texted me every now and again.

I wanted to respond when he sent the text that his professor finally allowed him back on the mat. He sent a selfie that had my body in knots. He was still so fine. He was also calm. I loved that for him.

Maybe he finally had what he needed to make better decisions. But what would happen if someone stepped on my shoe? Would he break their face for something trivial that he perceived as a threat? I couldn't waste time with the what-ifs. There were simply too many unknowns. Beyond the fuel to write sappy poems, going back and forth over Booker didn't help me in any way.

My graduation from the ultrasound program was around the corner. I was damn proud of myself. I accepted a job with the county hospital two weeks before school was out. They figured they wouldn't let their training be wasted for me to go and work somewhere else. Vince prepped me on how to negotiate my salary. I was grateful to have the offer while many of my classmates had no idea where they would work. Some of the clinical sites simply didn't have open positions.

The county hospital always needed help. Vince told me from the beginning I would get the worst shifts when I got hired. Each time he would say those things it made me feel like he had a lot of faith in my potential. New hires worked evenings, weekends, and overnights. But I didn't care. I wanted a nice place far from campus. Added pay on those shifts would help me earn what I needed and more.

I didn't accept the first dollar amount human resources offered like Vince instructed, and ended up making more than he did when he started several years back. He invited me out to celebrate, but I asked for a rain check. I wasn't ready for anything remotely romantic. Vince and I were friends, but there was a chance he would get the wrong impression. Whether I wanted to admit it or not, Booker was still in my heart.

My shifts for clinicals no longer felt like school. That damn hospital ran me ragged. But I had the bigger picture in mind. The more they sent me to do exams they hated, the more I learned. I showed up early and stayed late.

I finally spoke to my parents, and they were beside themselves with excitement over my graduation. I didn't want a party, but the dinner plans they coordinated were outrageous and the opposite of the low-key vibe I begged for. My little brother—who had graduated from high school and enrolled at the community college near our house for one semester—came to visit to prepare me for the shenanigans our parents had in store.

"What ever happened to old balls with the truck?" Fela asked as he flopped on my bed.

"Get up with your outside clothes on."

Fela got up and flopped on my chaise lounge in the same manner. I loved my brother, but he also annoyed the shit out of me sometimes.

"A few weeks ago, you was all MIA between school and ol' boy. What happened with him?"

"He has a record."

"No, shit."

"Watch your mouth."

"You broke up with him because he has a record?"

I didn't wanna have this conversation with my kid brother, but it seemed he wouldn't drop it otherwise.

"I knew he had a record. But I told him if he did anything that would get him sent back, we were done."

"He stole somethin'?"

"No."

"He hit you?" Fela stood and juice from the glass he held sloshed over the top.

"No, Fela! This why Mom make you eat everything in the dining room. You stay spilling shit."

"Y'all stay cleaning it up too," he mumbled.

More of his juice spilled when I slapped the back of his head.

"I'm not hearing the issue. I liked him."

I grabbed some laundry detergent and mixed it on a wet sponge and prayed it did the job. When I got back into my room, I handed it to Fela to clean up his own mess. He was right, we spoiled him.

"He took me to meet his family after he'd met y'all. Him and his cousin got into it. I told him we should leave because I knew he was a felon."

"Am I doin' this right?"

I nodded because the helpless act wouldn't work this time. He kept at it and the stain came up rather easily.

"I'm listenin'. What else happened?"

"I grabbed Trey's arm so we could go, but his cousin yanked me by the collar."

"Where he live?"

I tried to conceal my laughter. My little brother could fight, but he wasn't crazy enough to go look for trouble.

"Don't worry, Trey decided to pick him up and body slam him. I was fine with that, but when he crawled on top of him and punched him until his knuckles and shirt were covered in blood, I was done. It was way too much. It looked like something took over him, and he didn't snap out of whatever it was until I told him his aunt was calling the police." I turned to look at my brother and he had a goofy grin on his face.

"What could you possibly find funny about this? He could have gotten locked up again."

"He protected you. What more could a brother ask for?"

"Fela—"

"I get it. You're worried. But chances are he's racking his brain trying to figure out how to get you back. He'll think twice before he takes it too far next time."

"Next time?" I accepted the cleaning supplies from my brother and bent down to inspect his work.

He rolled his eyes upward at my need to double-check. "You know Mama is always preaching about showing grace. You didn't have a problem that he had a record in the first place. You need to cut him some slack."

I turned to leave the room.

"Before you end up another lonely Black wom—"

He didn't get to finish his sentence, because I turned around and kicked him in the butt.

"Damn, Sade. You and Trey belong together. Seriously though, sis, he beat up his own kinfolk for you. He loves you real big."

THE MORNING OF GRADUATION, I GOT ANOTHER TEXT FROM Booker.

*B.A.E: I know you read my messages. Thank God, you didn't block me. *sweating laughing emoji*

B.A.E: I just wanted to say how proud I am of you for finishing your ultrasound shit. D told me you graduate today.

B.A.E: His fiancée said we act like we're in a relationship and she's not sure how she feels about D stalking you for me.

B.A.E: I miss you, Sade

Me: I miss u too

He didn't text back. I figured he was stunned that I responded. We hadn't spoken in over a month. A lot had shifted since we last spoke. From the pictures and messages he sent, he seemed to be in a much better head space.

Booker told me he wasn't afraid he would get sent back anymore. I was relieved. I wanted to speak to him and be in his space again, but I was afraid. What if he made me regret it?

My mind was occupied with thoughts of Booker on the way to the stadium where graduation would be held. When I parked where I was instructed and ambled in the direction of the health science majors, my emotions were all over the place. I had finished my degree and already had a job lined up. My family was healthy and there was nothing I wanted. Except... him.

"Congratulations, number two," Brandon said when he saw me.

Brandon gave me a hard time because he was the smartest person in our cohort. It bugged me at first, but now that I knew I'd out-earn him he could keep that funky number-one spot.

"You're graduating and I heard you got a job? Why the long face?"

"News travels fast around here."

"Your guy told Miss Coleman how good you were months ago. He said if he had anything to do with it, the county hospital would hire you."

"Vince said that?"

"He sure did. Sounded like he had a thing for you."

"Whatever."

"What y'all talking about over here?" Imani asked as she and Jennifer wandered in our direction.

It made absolutely no sense to me why we were required to be at the ceremony an hour and a half early. This was a hurry-up-and-wait situation if I ever saw one.

"About how her county instructor is trying to bang."

"What grade are you in, Brandon?" Jennifer asked with irritation in her voice.

"I'm about to graduate from the sixteenth." He stuck his tongue out at her.

"I think you've spent too much time in pediatrics," I added.

"I just accepted a position, so this is my new normal."

"Who is that?" Imani asked. She fluffed her hair and pushed her breasts higher than they already sat in her barely there graduation dress.

"That's Sade's Vince," Brandon blurted.

"Hey, can I speak to you for a second?" Vince asked.

I always thought he was handsome, just not my type. Vince was the kind of man who had his entire life mapped out. And while I respected his goals, he was also the type of man who would seek to control an adventurous woman like me. I had to admit that he looked extra fine today with his plaid dress slacks and a fitted long-sleeved shirt. Not everyone could pull the look off the way he did.

Imani smacked her lips when I walked with Vince into the hallway next to the open room where the students were gathered. Little did she know I was only interested in one man, and things were complicated between us.

"You look beautiful as always," he started. Vince was nervous. "I just wanted to say congratulations." He leaned in to hug me and lingered for longer than necessary. When I pulled away, he kissed me.

When I stepped back, I blurted, "Vince, I'm with Trey." I wasn't sure where my admission came from. I didn't know where I stood with Booker, but my heart and my pussy still belonged to him.

"The ex-con?" The gruff tone of his voice was a huge turn-off and it made me uneasy. My gut told me he would hit me before Booker ever would.

I stepped back to create more space between us. "He's a human who was convicted of a crime. He still has a heart. What's so wrong with me being with him?"

Vince stared at me with his eyes squinted like he wanted to say more but he thought it best to choose his words carefully. "Is it serious?"

"It is for me."

Our heads flew down the hall where Booker stood with a bouquet of roses. My face lit up. Although I was afraid of what he might do to Vince, I felt safe again. He strolled in our direction full of confidence. Vince was handsome, but Booker was an ungodly grade of sexy. He took up space physically and mentally and it turned me on. Vince backed up because we all knew he didn't want it with Booker Avery Edmund III.

"Hey, baby," he said nonchalantly. His jaw was clenched, but it relaxed when he locked eyes with me. He leaned in and planted a heated kiss to my lips. "These still belong to me?" he asked as he handed me the flowers.

I nodded because he took my breath away.

He glared at Vince. "I really don't wanna have to fuck you up. I'll let you slide this time because you was just shootin' your shot. But if you kiss my lady again—"

"Baby," I started. I placed my hand on his chest to calm him. Vince walked away and mumbled something about how I wasn't worth it.

"What?" Booker was confused about why I interrupted him.

"I got a job at the county hospital. I still have to work with him."

Booker balled his fist tightly but relaxed when I leaned up and placed a kiss to his cheek.

"I'm glad you're here. Surprised, but happy."

"I couldn't wait to see you. So, I begged your teacher to tell me where you were."

"Miss Coleman told you where I was?"

He used his hands to stroke the stubble alongside his goatee and said, "I think she got a crush on me."

"Don't make me have to fuck my teacher up."

His eyes danced in playful delight. "You meant what you said to your new coworker about being with me?" Booker failed to hide his annoyance with Vince. I set the flowers down on a nearby table.

What he didn't know was when he hadn't responded to Vince with physical force, he stole my heart. If there was ever a time, I expected him to throw hands, it was the sight of another man's lips on mine. I would slap Miss Coleman into next week if she got anywhere near Booker's face. Booker Avery Edmund better known as Trey had demonstrated to me that he valued himself enough not to get sent back to prison.

I lifted my arms and wrapped them around his neck. His light brown skin—decorated with dark body ink—reddened under the contact.

"Did you mean it when you said it was serious for you?"

He looked me in my eyes and firmly replied, "Yes."

I kissed him like we weren't in a public place. I couldn't help the whimpers that escaped my lips whenever we kissed.

"Let me get a green light."

Booker wore a devious grin. *How the hell does he think we can handle business inside the auditorium?*

"What are you talking about?" I asked. Although I had a pretty good idea of what he wanted.

"Who is this?"

We separated slightly to see we had company. Jennifer startled the shit out of us. *Damn, these girls are nosey!* Jennifer and Imani stood and awaited my response.

"I'm Trey. It's nice to meet you both." He took Imani's hand and lifted it like he would kiss it. I'd seen him do that shit with Rashad's girl, and it wouldn't happen again. I slapped her hand out of his and they all laughed in response. I shrugged. He was mine and that was that.

"So, you're not with Vince?" Imani asked. This heffa was messy as hell.

"She's with me." Booker pulled me against his side like I'd get away if he didn't.

"I can introduce you," I added. Maybe Imani would get me back in Vince's good graces. The last thing I wanted was beef with the person who was probably responsible for getting me my job.

Imani clapped and bounced. When she did, her perky breasts bobbed uncontrollably. Booker was adorable. He looked everywhere but at Imani. I wasn't naive to think he wouldn't be attracted to other women, even I noticed her titties. But I'd be damned if he would kiss her hand.

"Where did you two meet?" Jennifer asked. She twirled her hair like we were in high school.

I faintly heard Booker tell her we met at the hospital. I took the opportunity to text Vince.

Me: *Hey, I know you're mad at me, but I can make it up to you*
Vince: *How?*

He responded quickly. Does he think I mean something freaky that will get us both killed?

Me: *My friend Imani wants to meet you*
Vince: *Which one?*

Me: *Lol, the one with the big breasts and wide eyes. She got a position at ENEP's medical center. She's a stunning nerd, kind of an airhead, but I think you'll like her*

Vince: *Is he treating you right?*

I sighed. I hoped to have this conversation once. But Vince had seen me when Booker and I were apart, and I was a mess. He may have gotten the impression we weren't right for each other, or that Booker did me dirty. That couldn't have been further from the truth.

Booker needed time and perspective to accept his hands weren't the only answer to every seemingly threatening situation.

Me: *Yes*

Vince: *Good. I'm on my way back*

"Imani. Vince is headed back to meet you."

She gasped and ran off. Booker and I looked at Jennifer to figure out what the hell just happened.

"She's going to fix her makeup and push up her boobs," Jennifer said with an enthusiastic tone.

"Damn," Booker whispered. I elbowed him in the ribs, and he laughed. "I'm just saying. You know her titties big as hell. How much more can she push them up?"

Less than two minutes after his text, Vince was on his way toward us. I felt Booker tighten beside me. They stared at each other while Jennifer and I stood awkwardly. She looked at her watch and announced that we had forty minutes before we needed to line up and she would catch up with us later. She didn't want part of whatever would pop off between Vince and Booker.

"Trey."

"Vince."

"Okay, boys. Here comes Imani," I added with a sterile smile plastered on my face.

"Imani, this is Vince. He is the student coordinator at the county hospital, and he taught me everything I know. He's been working there for about five years, so by my calculation, he's banking well over six figures—"

"That's plenty," Vince interjected.

Iman's eyes were wide and interested. She wasn't like me. She liked ultrasound, but she was willing to drop everything for the right man. That's why she chose the medical center. She said the person didn't have to be famous but needed to have a provider mindset. Vince fit the description.

"Hi, Vince. I'm Imani." She shifted her gaze to Booker and me.

"Trey, it was nice to meet you. I'll see you soon, Sade." She dismissed us, and I wasn't mad at her.

I picked up my flowers and walked Booker further into the hallway to give Imani and Vince space. The roses smelled divine. I couldn't wait to put them in a vase. I felt the heat from Booker's fit body behind me. "What's up with that green light?"

I craned my neck to look back at him. "Greenlight."

He sucked in a breath in anticipation. There was an office door at the end of the long hallway opposite the opening where students gathered. Booker grabbed my hand and guided me inside. He locked the door behind me.

"You have any idea how bad I missed you?" he asked. The words came out like he was in pain.

"Show me."

He lifted my Ivory-colored bodycon dress above my head. I'd taken extra care when I chose the matching bra and lace panty set—they were also white. I knew he appreciated what he saw by the way his hands were on my ass.

"We only have half an hour. Don't make me miss my graduation, Trey."

He slapped my ass, and the sting was delicious. "What I tell you about calling me Trey when I'm about to be knee-deep in this pussy?"

I removed my bra and boy-cut panties while I stared at him. "You told me not to, Trey."

He pulled his slacks and briefs off. I saw he remembered to bring protection this time. The thought of our first time together in his truck brought a smile to my face.

"I don't know why you're smiling. I'm giving you all of it."

For a moment, I wondered if he hadn't given me his entire length the first time. There was no way he didn't. He used the cardigan sweater that looked like it belonged to a professor to spread across the office desk. It was thoughtful how he wanted to protect my ass from a stranger's desk, but he would also pummel it like I'd stolen something —because I knew the right buttons to push with him. I may have needed someone direct who gave me the illusion of control, but Booker required a non-combative woman who challenged him every now and again—especially when it came to sex.

I sat at the edge of the desk and watched him take me in. There was nothing sexier than his attraction to every curve of my thick body.

"I got the green light to eat that pussy?" he asked as he neared the desk.

I shook my head. "I had something else in mind." I pulled his torso closer and grabbed his stiff manhood. It was as glorious as the day he came to the department for the ultrasound. I'd wanted to hold it in my hands and mouth then.

"I know what you trying to do. You trying to have me in here screaming like a bitch so your classmates can roast the shit out of me."

I heard him, but I paid Booker no mind. I opened my mouth slowly and lowered my head between his legs, where he stood in front of me. I breathed on his dick. It was a torture he deserved for our time apart. He gritted his teeth in anticipation. Just when his body relaxed, I closed my lips around his length. He swore up and down I tasted good, but the feel of him inside my mouth made my pussy leak.

I hummed on him, and his knees buckled.

"I'm getting your jacket wet. Having you in my mouth turns me on." I spoke between slurps and allowed for a pop sound each time I slipped him out of my mouth to speak.

"Fuck that jacket. I hope it smells like you. It'll hold me over until you get your diploma, and I can take you somewhere to properly fuck you. Shit!"

I read somewhere that if I squeezed the thumb of my left hand, it would suppress the gag reflex. I wasn't sure if the trick worked as a placebo or if there was merit, but by Booker's moans, I think it helped my head game.

"You like it?"

"Yeah, girl."

I knew Booker was a savage, but out of respect for me, he held back. It was a sign of commitment to keep me happy, but I wanted obscene sex with him. I moved my hands from his thigh and dick and grabbed his hands. I placed them on the back of my head. Naturally, he used his body and my head to fuck my mouth.

I felt pleasure and pressure build between my legs. I used my fingers to stroke my slick center and hummed again when Booker increased the pace of his movements. "I'm gonna marry your ass, Sade. These lips were made to be wrapped around my dick."

I liked it when he talked dirty to me. I was about to orgasm when he dropped his hands and stepped back. My mouth was tired, but I missed his presence immediately.

"I want you to cum while I'm inside of you."

"I wanted you to finish in my mouth," I whined.

Booker bit his bottom lip, and I could tell he liked my filthy mouth as much as I liked his. He linked my left thigh in the crease of his right arm and entered me hard. "I still got a green light?"

"Yes, Trey, dammit!"

He thrust into me roughly. Little did he know, that was how I liked it with him. I'd had rough sex in the past, but nothing anywhere near what Booker was capable of. The insecure, possessive man who thought he could fuck me into submission wasn't my thing. Booker didn't have to try hard for me to fall in line, and that was when he wasn't far in the depths of my center like he was now.

"What you call me?" He lifted my leg higher, and his dick tapped my walls from a different angle. I came loud. My back arched and my ass raised off the desk that was covered with his cardigan.

"Booker!" I was sure the entire graduating class heard my wails. I couldn't care less.

He placed his hand over my mouth and continued his pleasurable torment. He slowed his pace but kept his strokes deep.

"You fuckin' right. Nobody else in the world can call me that. But your fuck voice is so sexy, I want to hear it every time I'm in this pussy."

"Yes, daddy." My words were muffled under his hand, but it didn't matter.

He lifted my other leg. Both of my legs rested in the creases of his arms.

"Did you miss my body, Booker?"

"You know I did. I couldn't even beat my meat. I waited weeks 'cause I knew it would be worth it once I got you back."

"For real?" I wanted to believe what he said was game and merely because he liked how he felt when he was inside me, but the seriousness of his glare and tone told me he meant what he said. He'd gone with no sex and no masturbation while we were apart. That made one of us because I pleasured myself several times when my body ached for him despite my mind's refusal to go and be with him.

I grabbed my ankles and lifted them from his arms and further into the air.

"Shit, Sade. I'm about to cum."

"Wait."

Booker stilled and I felt awful. He said he wanted to use safe words for this very reason. I released my legs and stood. I placed a quick kiss on his cheek, turned, and tooted my ass up in his face. "I'm sorry, baby. I didn't mean 'red'. I meant for you to hit it from the back first."

He released a sigh of relief. "I'm glad you did. Because your ass is magnificent."

Booker reached his hand between us. When I craned my head to see him, the same fingers moved to the space between his lips. Our eyes connected, and for the first time, I had no doubt Booker had taken up residence in my heart. I was hesitant to make plans with him the way I wanted because of his record. He said he wasn't on the hunt for a surrogate mother, but how could he support himself with a felony?

My head was concerned with that, but apparently, my heart and body were all in. I smirked at him, and he responded with his hand against the side of my face until it was smashed against his jacket where my juices were. He entered me in a slow, sensual manner. I didn't want slow. I wanted Booker so deep in my pussy I was left with no choice but to climb the damn walls.

I twerked my ass and bounced it against him. He slapped my cheeks, and it only fueled my lust and possible love for him. Booker spread my cheeks apart and entered me slowly and easily. Once I adjusted to his depth, he thrusted harder. I cried out, undeterred by where we were.

Booker was my graduation present. I would whimper and moan as loud as I wanted. My phone was set to vibrate, but the sound was loud enough to get my attention.

"Fuck your phone."

I knew if I didn't help him along, Booker would continue to take all the time he needed. I had no idea how long we'd been at it, and I wanted to walk with the other students at graduation. I put my fingers in my mouth to wet them. I shifted my gaze to make sure he saw me. Then I reached my hands between us and stroked his balls.

It was his undoing. He slammed into me four more times before he roared and came undone. He rested his weight against my backside and flicked my nipple ring when he did.

"You rushed me," he said between breaths.

"I told you that you're not the boss of me."

He gave my satiated pussy a smack. It sent aftershocks through my body as I reached for my phone. When I saw the screen of my phone, I burst into laughter.

Brandon Smartass: We heard you and your Booker from clear across the hallway

"What's that about?" Booker asked as he separated from me. There was a bathroom connected to the office where I saw him go to clean himself up.

"It's Brandon. The other guy from my class."

"What's up with him?"

"He said they all heard us. But apparently, Imani had our back.

She played music to distract them and get them to focus on the turn-up that's poppin' off after the ceremony."

He returned with dampened paper towels for me. I could do my best, but the way Booker made my pussy leak, I'd be soggy for the rest of the night.

"You embarrassed?"

I was distracted by the sight of his muscular thighs. He slipped back into his outfit like he hadn't just done those unspeakable acts to me. I, on the other hand, was frazzled. I doubted I'd be able to walk the line without remnants of this orgasm.

"Hell no. Now if my legs are too weak to get my diploma, then I'll be embarrassed."

He leaned in and kissed me. My phone vibrated in my hand, and he swiped it from me. My heart dropped. I explained to him that a little playful jealousy was fine, but if he was about to tell Brandon to stop texting me, we were gonna have an issue. He kissed me deeper, then returned the phone to my hand.

"I just wanted your full attention while I kissed you."

It was another text from Brandon. He said I had fifteen minutes to get in line before they filed out. Booker felt me up a little more and told me he'd try to contain himself until we were alone again, but he wouldn't make any promises.

I joined my classmates, aware that everyone knew what I'd been up to. I pretended to be aloof, but I felt the stares of envy from the other girls in my class. I would be jealous too. The way Booker put it on me, he had me willing to change my name to Sade Edmund.

11

Trey

My dad was the only one who seemed to notice the satisfied look on my face when I sat down on the bleachers with him and the rest of my people. I invited everybody because I wanted Sade to know how much she meant to me. It was my grand gesture. I was caught off guard at how quickly she gave me the green light.

I had no idea how long I'd been gone. Sade asked me to hang on to her flowers while she did her thing. I got smiles from women both young and old when they saw me with them, but my dad stared at them and frowned at me.

"What?"

He wrinkled his brows again. "Where you been?"

"I gave Sade her flowers."

My mother and aunt chuckled. They knew what I meant. I'm sure no one expected her to carry them across the stage.

"I see you're in a good mood."

It was an observation, but so what? I *was* in a good mood. I'd been as nervous as a groom on his wedding day when we arrived. I didn't know what to expect. Sade could have told me to step off. When I saw Vince put his lips on hers, I saw red. I was furious and the urge to destroy him was strong, but I focused my attention on my lady.

Sade didn't like him any more than she liked pickles on a sandwich. He couldn't see it, but I did. I stood and watched them together in the hallway, when all I had to bank on was her earlier text that she missed me. She announced we were together when we hadn't technically made up yet. There was nothing that could knock the smile off my face.

"How much longer?" I asked. Sade told me it was time for them to line up. Where were they?

"You know these things take time," my Aunt Nae teased.

I huffed and looked at my watch. There was at least fifteen minutes before they even filed out. My phone rang with an unknown number. I was tempted not to answer, but my curiosity got the best of me.

"Hello."

"Trey?"

I recognized Jamie's voice right away. I thought about her a lot. I didn't regret what I did to Sean, but I often wondered how my violence affected her. If I had the words to say at the time, I would have asked if she was okay. I wouldn't have done it right in front of her. I prayed she didn't feel responsible for his death because it wasn't her fault. It was his and mine alone.

"Jamie?"

My mom and dad both heard. My dad's knee bounced uncomfortably, and my mom rubbed my back in support. Her and Aunt Nae's eyes watered. I stood to excuse myself and moved to an area where I could hear her clearly.

"Wow. I didn't expect you to know who I was so quickly." Her voice was tiny like she was.

"Of course, I would."

"Why did you do it?"

I swallowed. Jamie got right to the point. No warm-up or anything. What the hell was I supposed to say? He asked for it.

"I mean, it's not like we were that close," she pressed.

"It didn't matter. You were thirteen." My throat burned and I briefly wondered if I could get to the academy without letting Sade down for leaving the ceremony. Physical force was my superpower, I just had to be wise about the way I used it. I could hear her breath, but she didn't speak.

"I'm glad you're out. I felt awful when I heard about your sentence."

"Thank you. I wouldn't wish it on anybody, but I think I needed the time to learn more about the way I'm wired. There's a lot of different ways I could have responded."

"You wish he was alive?"

"Hell no!" I said forcefully. "I mean... I wish I would have checked on you and told you nothing that happened was your fault. And I regret that you saw it."

"Oh. Is it bad that I miss him?"

Fuck! Jamie needed somebody to speak to. Somebody more qualified with this type of shit than me. I knew I couldn't live my life with hate in my heart for Sean, but what he'd done to her was unforgivable. I wouldn't budge on that. I could only imagine how many times he'd done it and how long it had gone on for him to not even lock the doors.

"I miss him too."

"I've thought about what happened to me a lot since I moved. Thank you, Trey."

"For what?"

"Doing something."

I had a headache. She still sounded like the shy little girl who always begged us to play with her dolls. Sean was the only one who would.

"What do you mean?"

"You weren't the only one who saw. But nobody did anything. At the time, I figured if adults didn't do anything maybe it wasn't bad."

"It was bad, and it was wrong. But, Jamie, if you never remember anything from this call, I need you to know you didn't do anything to deserve what happened to you or what I did to Sean."

"Thank you, Trey." Her voice broke a little, but she regained her composure. "Are you at a game or something?" I heard Jamie's smile through the phone. The families of the graduates were rowdy and excited for the ceremony to begin. Music played through the speakers to keep them at bay, but their patience was thin.

"I'm at my girlfriend's graduation."

"Girlfriend?"

If my memory serves me right, Jamie should graduate from high school this year.

"Yeah. If you're ever up to it, I would love for you to meet her."

"I'll let you know."

"Okay. Jamie?"

"Yeah, Trey?"

"I'm glad you called. Take care of yourself."

"I will."

The call disconnected. She would never know the amount of closure her words gave me. I was able to answer her questions that sounded like they'd bothered her for years. And she thanked me. My soul needed that.

The graduation started with old ass people who made long, dry speeches. I caught Sade turn her head to locate me. I flicked my tongue out at her and knew by the way she fidgeted in her chair she was wet again already. Her family sat near where my crew was. Some of them were apprehensive to sit in our row. When there were more than a handful of Edmund's in one place our energy intimidated outsiders. We weren't street by any means. We were hood adjacent.

When we filed in, I gave Fela a pound. He said he was just happy that his sister would finally stop moping. D and his lady and Rashad and his girl came. I think they felt invested in our relationship since D stalked Sade for me when she stopped responding to my texts. He was the one who told me when and where the graduation was.

"It's about time," my dad said when they lined the students up to call their names. I elbowed him because he made fun of me when I was restless.

My heart was in my stomach. I hadn't known Folasade for long, but I wanted her in my life. I knew if I told her, there was a chance she'd push me away. She was honest about the men who tried to control her in the past. I wanted to possess her body, but only if she said green. The man who read the names finished the C last names and started with D.

I think I held my breath until it was her turn.

"Folasade Amira Dixon, Summa Cum Laude."

Our entire section roared with applause. We hooted and hollered to the point that other families joined in. She got the loudest support of the night. Her likeness was on the monitor for the auditorium to see. I could see the confusion on her pretty face. Her smooth skin begged me to lick it.

Along with my talk with Miss Coleman, I jumped through every hoop possible to get the administration to agree to withhold Sade's diploma. The noise died down as people started to wonder what the holdup was. Graduations were already long as hell and they'd only gotten to the D last names.

"I love you, Sade," I yelled once everyone was quiet.

She wore the biggest smile on her face when she realized it was me. She found me and mouthed that she loved me too. There were awwws from the women in attendance, but I'd just gotten started.

With purposeful strides, I made my way to the stage. Once I was in front of her, I dropped to one knee. Her mouth fell open and for two seconds I was distracted with lewd images of Sade and that mouth. The man with the poofy hat and black robe cleared his throat.

"Okay. I only have ten seconds to spill my guts before they play the music or toss me out."

Sade laughed nervously.

I pulled the blue box from my cardigan and opened it. The diamond shined and I saw a few of the teachers on stage stand up to see it better. I'd done a damn good job with the selection of her flawless emerald-cut diamond engagement ring. My palms were sweaty, but I maintained my cool on the outside.

"I want to give you the life you deserve. You got your dream job and if you give me a greenlight, I'll do whatever I can to be your dream husband. I'm not perfect. I have a bit of a temper when it comes to the safety of the people I love. But you taught me how important it is to protect your heart with the same intensity I would your body."

She smirked at me, and I lost focus once again.

"The professor gave me the academy. I knew not to ask questions when he had me in meetings with accountants and lawyers and when he made me do maintenance around the place. First, I had no idea how much money the gym was worth, and second, I didn't realize he was ready to retire. He gave it to me and an advance. I can take care of you however you want now—financially, physically, sexually."

The man cleared his throat louder and people in the audience laughed.

"I'm sorry," I said toward the crowd. "Will you be my wife, Sade?"

I held my breath. She told me not to lock her down. She told me she needed freedom, and she didn't want to be controlled. Sade also said she wanted a man to lead and take charge. My proposal was just that. It was our time.

She nodded and tears streamed down her round face.

"Yeah?"

"Yes, Trey!"

I was so excited, I forgot where we were. The moment she let me put my ring on her finger I lifted her into my arms and kissed her like I'd die without her. The crowd cheered and I attempted to walk off stage.

"My diploma," she said in my ear. I couldn't hear shit over the applause.

"I'm gonna let that Trey slide because we're in public," I said inches from her lips.

I ambled in the direction of the man who allowed me to take over his ceremony and he handed Sade her diploma. "Congratulations, you two."

SADE

DINNER WAS AMAZING. BOTH OUR FAMILIES GOT ALONG WELL. Booker was the calmest I'd ever seen him be. Another patron bumped him on the way in and he asked if the other person was all right.

He sat across from me and kept his eyes on me throughout the meal. No matter who he conversed with, his eyes would find me. He'd give me a wink or blow me a kiss. Fela made fun of him, and he simply shrugged.

"I love her, man. I can't help it."

I listened to Booker as he told my dad about the Jiu Jitsu academy and his professor. He owned a gym, and apparently had put offers on a few homes near the county hospital.

"It's not the safest area," I said when he mentioned where the homes were.

"It is when I'm your man."

The table went silent. Booker's voice was deadly serious. The glare on his face told me all I needed to know. I had no doubt he'd kill for me. It made me feel safe, turned on, and a little worried all at once.

"Okay then, nephew," his Aunt Nae said. She broke the tension among everyone. It was one of the many reasons I liked her. That and she told me stories about how cute Booker's butt was when he was a baby.

Imani called to thank me for the introduction to Vince. She said she hoped to be where I was in a few months. She said she was relieved that Vince didn't seem jealous when Booker proposed. Imani said even though he was several chairs away from her with the other instructors, his attention had been on her breasts while Booker was on stage with me.

I wasn't sure why she felt the titty part was a good thing, but if she liked it, I loved it. I mostly listened while Booker chatted with my family. Every now and again, I would feel the weight of my new ring and my eyes would water. I loved Booker, but I had no clue he felt this deeply for me.

He asked my dad's permission in advance, which I thought was an antiquated practice and completely unnecessary. I could tell how much it meant to my dad though. I'd celebrated myself with them enough. I was ready for something else.

I removed my shoe and slipped my foot between Booker's legs. He choked on his spit and tried to keep up with his conversation with his dad. I felt his dick get hard instantly. I loved how powerful I felt with him. It also amused me how flustered he was as my toes rubbed against his length.

"Yellow," he said to me.

So, I slowed the movement of my foot. He removed his cardigan and placed it in his lap.

"Could you excuse us for a second? Sade, may I speak with you for a moment?"

"Sure. What's up, Trey?" I sat with a smirk on my face as he rounded the table. His jaw was clenched, and I knew there was only so much he could say or do in front of our folks.

"I'm just going to borrow you, baby. It won't take long."

His long fingers stroked the naked skin of my shoulders.

"Why can't you just do what he asked?" Fela said as if he was on

Booker's side of the family. The amount of irritation in my brother's voice let me know where his loyalty was.

I stood and noted Booker still had the cardigan in front of him. He was hard and wanted to hide it. He wrapped his arm around my neck and let his hand drop in front of my breast. As we walked, he let his fingers skim my cleavage. I moaned.

The sexual tension between us was off the charts. We stood in the small hallway of bathrooms in search of a place to get down. He was much too territorial for us to use the men's room, and I was afraid one of our moms would catch us in the women's. Booker surveyed our surroundings, and when he was confident we were alone, he pulled me into the family restroom.

As soon as he locked the door behind me, he pressed the front of my body against the wall and lifted my dress. His hands slipped beneath my panties, where he found my center as slick as it was before graduation. Booker didn't speak, but his rough breaths communicated plenty. I'd gotten him riled up with my under-the-table foot action and refusal to call him anything but Trey.

He snatched down my ruined panties. I was on the verge of an orgasm already. I heard him undo his pants and I held my breath expectantly. He lined himself up with my center from behind me and pushed his dick inside of me with a vengeance. I was gone off one stroke. I cried out from my fierce orgasm until I felt his rough hand cover my mouth.

"You gon' let me shoot the club up?" he asked between thrusts.

I couldn't believe my ears. Booker wanted a wife, and now he wanted children. I wasn't ready to be a mother, but in time I would gladly have his fighting-ass kids. I mumbled beneath his hand.

When he removed it, he asked again. "Can I make you my wife and my baby mama?"

I giggled. He felt too good. His words had my mind in a different space than my body. He pushed my back, so I was forced to lean forward then slapped my ass when I did.

"What's funny?"

"If I'm your wife, I can't be your baby mama."

"Who says? I want you to have my kids, my money, and my name."

He picked up his pace. His rough hands held my hips tightly as he went to work.

"You want that, Sade?"

"Yeah, Trey."

He squeezed my pierced nipple with enough pressure to elicit a second orgasm.

"What did you call me?"

"I could call you Prison Bae."

He slapped my ass again and continued deep strokes as he stood behind me.

"Like that shit you have me saved as in your phone, because of my initials?"

"Yep."

"You wanna be fucked like I just got out?"

"Yes, Booker. Please!"

"Grab your muthafuckin' ankles," he commanded. His voice was forceful, and my pussy purred.

I did as I was told. Booker pulled my cheeks apart and pushed into me at a tortuously slow pace. He reached in front of me and squeezed my clit.

"I don't think I can cum again and have the ability to walk."

"I can carry you, baby."

I knew he liked his balls stroked, and I'd successfully rushed him a few hours ago. I wet my fingers in my mouth and reached my hand between us to tickle his balls.

"Shit, Sade."

A knock on the door startled us but didn't stop Booker's movement nor did it stop my hands from the torture I inflicted between his legs. He thrust a few more times before he silently moaned in relief.

"Give us a second," he mumbled.

"I knew y'all freaky asses was in here," Fela said in disgust. "Mom and Dad are looking for y'all for pictures. Hurry it up," he said and walked off.

I laughed, and Booker joined me. "You think he still likes you?" I asked as I stood to face him.

"Yeah. He thanked me for protecting you. That's all I would want for my cousins."

"I know, baby."

Booker cleaned himself up and regarded me in the mirror. "I want you to have my kids."

"Kids?"

"Yes, girl. Can you do that?"

"I'd like to have you to myself for a while, but yeah I'll be your baby mama," I teased.

He slapped me on my ass and helped me get decent so we could face our folks after some of the best public sex I'd ever had.

EPILOGUE

T rey

I was the happiest man in the world. Sade had finally agreed to move in with me before the wedding, and things couldn't be better at the gym. Professor Sebastian stayed around to help me with the transition for two months until he said it was time to cut the cord. Enrollment had never been higher, and I felt like I continued his legacy to set other Black men free like his ancestors said he would.

Sade worked a lot, and I was mostly OK with it. We would have a problem if she got pregnant and refused to slow down. Not only did she stand for the duration of most of her shifts, but they wanted her to lift heavy patients while she was there. We didn't discuss the testicle exams anymore because it always led to a fight. I didn't want her to do them no matter how much they paid, but she agreed to avoid inmates.

The house wasn't ready. It would be finished by the end of the week. I wanted Sade to see what I'd done to our bedroom. I hired a local artist to do a mural above where our bed would go. I hoped she loved it as much as I did. I heard her car in the driveway, and I got butterflies like I always did when she was near me. It didn't matter if she gave me the silent treatment or if she was on her way to me for some midday sex, I was always excited to be in her space.

I loved Sade, and I couldn't wait to start a family with her. I hadn't been prepared for her to challenge me as much as she did outside of the bedroom. She meant it when she said she needed the illusion of freedom. We butted heads about the definition of what freedom looked like. For her, it meant she checked in when she felt like it. To me, it meant if she was my lady like she said she was, I worried about her when she didn't call or text after she left work.

A couple of times, she met with other classmates for drinks. I knew she wouldn't cheat on me, and I truly wanted her to have a life outside of what we had going on, but I hadn't spoken to her since she left for work that morning. Sade didn't speak to me for days after I had her brother call her to see if she was okay. Other than that, I had no complaints. Sex with her was never boring. Most of the time, we got down in public. We went at it wherever the hell we were and when the mood hit us.

When we were at her place or mine, we talked and spent nonphysical time together. I would have sex with Sade five times a day if she let me, but those moments where she filled me in on her work or we laid on the couch and watched her favorite show had become just as fulfilling. Now that I was at the academy six days a week, I'd only been on the verge of a blackout once. Someone new to my neighborhood stepped to Sade while she was on her way in to see me. When she turned him down, he got salty and grabbed her by the elbow. My lady was thick and therefore he must have put excessive force behind the pull to make her stumble.

I calmly walked out the front door and asked if she was okay. And when I punched him in the face, I was fully in my body. I didn't black out and I didn't go overboard like I had with Chris, but his ass needed to know she had me if he tried it again. He would think twice before he even said hello to her. I knew I'd done good because Sade sucked my dick like the freak she was once we were inside.

"Baby, I'm home," Sade said from downstairs.

She teased me about it, but I loved it when she announced herself. She came home to me. I descended the steps two at a time to greet her.

I pressed my lips to hers and grabbed her booty like we hadn't woken up together in her apartment.

"Why's your ring around your neck?"

"We had to help with a surgery today and I couldn't keep it on."

I blew out a breath because I didn't want to start a fight. The surgeon who did the ultrasound-assisted surgery said some slick shit about how beautiful she was and how he wanted her there with him so he could perform better. Sade felt like if I trusted her, I shouldn't be pressed. I wanted to see his ass in person. Apparently, he'd already had affairs with several nurses and x-ray techs.

She held my head between her hands and kissed me deeply.

"What's that for?"

"For dropping it. I know it's not easy focusing on me and what we have when there are so many distractions. Randall is a distraction."

"Who the hell is Randall?"

"Dr. Westin."

She pulled me close to her because I was tight about this man who was obviously interested in my future baby mama.

"Y'all on a first-name basis now?"

"He bought lunch for the department and told us to call him Randall."

I bit my tongue to keep from ruining our time together. If I said what I thought about him, it would lead to an argument. I turned and motioned for her to follow me to the bedroom. I knew Sade was loyal, but I couldn't help but feel disrespected when people came at her sideways.

"If it helps, I got the impression Vince doesn't like him either. He asked about you and referred to you as my fiancé."

I smiled at her. "I appreciate him. Him and Imani must be doing well."

"They are gross. Cute, but gross. Is that how we look to other people?"

As we reached the top of the stairs, I asked, "What you mean?"

"Every time she comes to the office, all we hear is lips and ass smacking. And when he comes back to work, he has the same goofy grin you have after you feel me up."

"I guess. I don't give a damn what other people think."

When she entered the room, her mouth dropped open. And damn if I didn't want to put my dick inside it.

"Booker, what did you do?"

"I had a picture of the most beautiful thing in the world painted on our wall. I want to see it first thing in the morning and right before I fall asleep at night."

"My ass?" She swatted me and laughed.

"It's not just your ass. Your face and titties are in it too."

"What if my parents see this?"

"We grown. They need to stay out of grown folks' business." She swatted me again. "You want me to change it?"

"I didn't say all that."

I turned to face her and pulled her into my arms. "Thank you."

"For what?"

"For giving me my life back. If it wasn't for you, I know I woulda got locked up again. I wouldn't be doing something useful with my life. I'm helping Black boys without dads and kids with anger issues."

She leaned up and kissed me. "I love you, Trey."

My dick responded to her words. She knew I associated her referral to me by my nickname as a challenge. "You know what that does to me, and you do it anyway."

"Yep. I fired all the security at my pussy's club."

"I can shoot the club up?"

"Greenlight."

The End

AFTERWORD

Thank you for finishing *Prison Bae*.

If you enjoyed this story, **leave me a five-star review on Amazon, and a positive review on Goodreads,** and **TikTok.** And recommend it to your friends.

Also, I share freebies, sneak peeks, and discounts for sensual products on my mailing list! Sign up here.

http://eepurl.com/h15QoD

Thank you in advance,
Denise Essex

Sweet Heat
DENISE ESSEX

ALSO BY DENISE ESSEX

More *Sweet Heat* Reads by Denise 💋

The Firemen's Ball: A Masquerade Affair
My Book

The Pleasure Package
https://bit.ly/pleasurepackage

A Naughty Rendezvous
https://bit.ly/ANaughtyRendezvous

Love in the same strip club
https://bit.ly/SameStripClub

Heat Haven Heaux-Tell: Three Novellas
https://bit.ly/HeatHaven

The College Route
https://bit.ly/TheCollegeRoute

I Found Her
https://amzn.to/3VmWLm7

The Visiting Professor
https://bit.ly/TheVisitingProfessor

Gone For a Soldier

https://bit.ly/GoneForASoldier

LET'S CONNECT!

Where to find me in these intanet streets 💋

https://linktr.ee/deniseessex